Cinderella
Dreams
of Fire

by Casey Lane

CINDERELLA DREAMS OF FIRE

Book cover designed by Omri Koresh.
Typography designed by Lee Dignam.
Edited by Ashley Gainer Lankford.

www.caseylanebooks.com

Thanks From Casey

I absolutely need to thank some folks who made this book possible. I couldn't have done this without the help of Sheridan Stancliff, Ashley Lankford, Lee Dignam, Paula Pettit Skender, Laura Martone, Cameron Scott Wright, Penelope Campbell-Myhill, Cameron Jace, K.M. Shea, and many others who assisted along the way.

After receiving so much help, I hope that I can give back a little. Check out the offer below if you'd like to get a hold of my free novella. Thanks again!

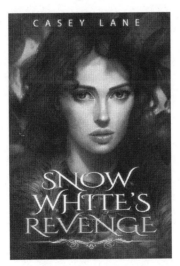

She's a prisoner. He wants an adventure. Together, they'll change a kingdom forever. Get a free ebook edition of *Snow White's Revenge* by joining Casey's email list.

Visit http://bit.ly/caseylanelist to get your free book!

PART 1

CHAPTER 1

The cold night air made Kiyara shiver, and she wondered what she and her family would need to do to survive. She looked up at the lantern outside the old, broken-down inn. She hoped it would be warm inside. Kiyara hoped her mother wouldn't have to do anything drastic to keep them safe.

Armenia's fingernails pressed through her quaking daughter's too-thin cloak and into her shoulders. "Stay close to me, my dears. This land isn't like our own."

Kiyara was actually glad to hear that, since they'd almost been murdered in their own home.

Her mother opened the door, causing an ancient creak to seep into the blackness of night. A musty odor mixed with alcohol met Kiyara's nose as they stepped into the light. They hadn't been to many taverns as a family, but she assumed that most of them were just as dirty, impersonal, dimly lit, and with at least one passed-out drunk near the kegs.

She had the feeling of unfamiliar eyes meeting them from all sides.

Kiyara glanced at Malina. They were both dressed in similarly drab cloaks, though her sister somehow made hers look much less depressing. The tattered garb was a far cry from the tailored clothes they wore in the royal castle. While Kiyara imagined her own eyes were filled with fear, her sister seemed to have something else on her mind. Whatever it was, it only made Kiyara's distress increase.

An innkeeper entered the main room from the back. He looked as old and grizzled as the tavern itself. Perhaps a little less dirty, but not by much.

Their mother left them beside the drunk and glided over to the man of the house.

Kiyara watched Malina dart her head from side to side before grabbing

1

the man's drink and swigging from it. Her sister gagged at the taste and slammed the mug down. Kiyara wished she could shrink so small that no one would ever see her again.

Her mother leaned across the bar, as if to put her chest on display for the innkeeper. "Good evening."

The man spit on the ground. "Not sure why you brought children in here, but it's not safe for them."

She licked her lips. "Few places are these days. Who owns most of the land in this area?"

The innkeeper narrowed his eyes. "Strange question to be asking late at night."

"Does it have a strange answer?"

"I'm guessing it's the earl. He's a good man. Better than most."

Kiyara watched her mother lean even closer to the man, who smelled vaguely of rotten fish. "The earl wouldn't happen to be looking for partnership, would he?"

The innkeeper's grim face grew darker. "I'm happy to let you and your girls get a few minutes out of the cold, but this is no place for families and I'm not one to answer such odd questions at this time of night."

"Father?"

A young girl entered the room. She wore similar clothing to the man behind the bar, which easily painted them as related. She seemed as if she hadn't bathed in days, which normally would've made Kiyara uncomfortable, but she and her sister had barely touched water in the last month. She shuddered to think what the girl thought of the three of them.

Part of her wanted to shout, "We were princesses, I swear." But she remained silent.

The innkeeper's face warmed slightly. "Go to bed, Brianne, my love. I'm closing up soon."

Kiyara's mother looked at the girl like a snake eyeing its prey. "What a beautiful daughter. I'm sure my Malina would just love playing with her."

With a nod, Malina pulled back her cloak and wrenched a dagger from her boot. Before the innkeeper could make a sound, Kiyara's sister had the blade pointed at the girl's throat.

Kiyara's mouth twitched. Everything felt so familiar.

2

The little girl let out a mousey squeak. "Father!"

Malina pressed the dagger tighter against the girl's neck. "Quiet, or it goes deeper. And then you bleed."

Kiyara backed away and tripped over the drunken man's shoe. As she fell to the ground, she heard the innkeeper rummaging through his pockets.

"Please, leave my daughter alone! I'll answer anything you want, I swear. The earl lives a few miles east of here. He's married. Has a daughter the same age as mine. Just please, leave my family out of this!"

Kiyara was almost glad she didn't have to see what was about to unfold. She knew Armenia was past the point of gathering information. Her mother was hungry.

Kiyara glanced up to see Malina move the dagger down and slice at the girl's arm. Her sister laughed as the girl cried out.

The innkeeper's voice shook. "She's all I have left. You can stay here as long as you like. You can have the entire place if you want it."

Her mother drew out every last syllable. "I don't want your tavern. I don't even want your daughter. I want something more."

Kiyara saw the red, magical light reflected on the stone of the ceiling. She shut her eyes tight.

Make it stop. Please, make it stop.

She didn't have to look to know exactly what was happening. Even though her eyes were shut, she knew her mother had laid her hands on the innkeeper's chest.

Kiyara sobbed silently as she listened to the young girl scream and the innkeeper beg for his life.

She rocked herself on the ground. "We're going to be okay. We're going to be okay."

CHAPTER 2

Cinderella scrubbed at the stone floor where she used to play with her dolls over a decade ago. Her pruned hands worked the brush to get out every last drop of the dark wine stain.

She didn't remember what her toys looked like. She barely even recalled the proud face of her mother looking down upon her, the joyful daughter. There was no joy anymore. There was only cleaning and getting ready for the day when she would break the chains.

Until that time, however, every moment she passed in what used to be her father's beautiful house would be spent smelling of soap and oils.

"Could be worse. Could be ash."

Even though Cinderella's stepsister Malina was the one who snuck into her mother's stash and proceeded to spill the dark purple liquid all over the ground, Cinderella received the blame. Armenia wasn't her mother, and she'd played the role as horribly as possible for the last decade or so. Ever since the woman had stormed into their lives and swept up the mourning, debilitated earl.

Of course, Cinderella hated Armenia, but she saved a different breed of contempt for her father. If he ever spoke to her again, she would consider letting him know about it.

She heard light tiptoes from the other side of the hallway. Most normal people wouldn't have picked up on it. Most normal people hadn't spent every night for 10 years training their senses.

Cinderella raised her voice as she kept her head down. "I hear you, Kiyara. No need to sneak around. You didn't do this."

She heard a long sigh before her other stepsister made herself known.

Kiyara and her sister both looked like their mother's daughters, but

4

they couldn't wear those looks more differently. While Malina used her ample bosom and long, flowing hair to string all the noblemen along, Kiyara took similar attributes and made them kind and gentle. She looked every bit a princess, while her sister seemed more likely to stab a princess in the back.

Kiyara slouched, as if she wanted to look smaller and less significant. "I'm sorry, Elle. I should've kept an eye on Malina. She really is impossible."

Cinderella attempted a vigorous scrub of the last remaining patch of wine. The stain was not cooperating.

"She isn't your responsibility. According to your mother, anything she does to upset her pristine house is all on me."

Kiyara looked up and sighed anew. "It isn't fair."

"Tell me something I don't know."

A half-smile formed on her stepsister's face. "We're going to meet the prince soon. There's a tea followed by a ball a little later. Maybe Mother will let you go."

Cinderella laughed. "A ball. I remember before my father turned into a mute and married a beast, no offense of course, we used to go to all sorts of parties." She tried in vain to remember her mother's face as they danced in circles so many years ago. "But I wasn't of age back then. Maybe the prince will take a shine to you."

Kiyara blushed. "Me? He would never look at me with my sister around."

Cinderella pushed off the floor. There was no way all the wine was coming out. "You never know. Some people have a pretty low tolerance for evil."

They laughed until they heard the heavy steps of Armenia two floors above them. She wasn't big on laughter. Or sounds of any kind, really.

Kiyara shrunk herself back down again. "I have to go. We're going into town to be fitted for our ball gowns. I'll see if I can get a fourth one made for you."

Cinderella cracked her knuckles. "As much as I appreciate your optimism, Kiyara, you have about as much a chance of getting that fourth dress as I do of getting this stain all the way out."

"I guess that's what makes me an optimist."

They smiled at each other before Kiyara turned and walked away.

Cinderella no longer minded the cleaning so much. After all, she'd been forced to do it since the day of her father's second wedding. She still remembered picking up after all the guests as if she were the hired help. Seeing the earl get married again so soon after her mother had died made her angry and upset enough. Being treated like a slave took things to a whole new level.

Over time, the water-soaked hands and achy knees didn't hurt nearly as much as the time devoted to her own thoughts. She endlessly replayed countless embarrassing moments from her adolescence. Her stepmother kicking her into a puddle of mud in front of her former school classmates and Malina torturing her with no sleep during a particularly trying week in her early teens bubbled to the top. But Cinderella no longer had to worry about sleep. She only needed the couple of hours before dawn after prowling the village at night.

She heard the front door close, followed by the carriage taking the earl's wife and "his two lovely daughters" into town. Cinderella glanced up to the ceiling just below her father's study. She couldn't remember the last time he'd spoken a word to her. It was possible that she hadn't even seen him since Kiyara snuck him downstairs for her 16th birthday.

Two whole years ago.

Cinderella walked over to the window and opened it to let the air dry the wet stone inside. The cool breeze reminded her of her late-night dashes across the village, with the wind whipping in her hair as she leapt from rooftop to rooftop. Her legs instinctively crouched as if she were about to make a particularly difficult jump.

A sound from outside caught her attention, and with lightning-quick speed, she extended her hand at just the right moment. A small rock wrapped in parchment made impact with her palm and she closed her fingers around it.

Cinderella glanced outside, but she never saw where the notes came from. She only knew who sent them.

She unwrapped the string and spread out the parchment on the wall. A quick scan gave her a location and an item. She didn't know who the object belonged to, but it wouldn't be theirs much longer.

She smiled to herself. "I'll clean your house now, Armenia. But the second you go to sleep, I'm not yours anymore."

Cinderella crumpled the parchment and made to start a small, evidence-destroying fire.

"Tonight, I work for the Godmother."

CHAPTER 3

Braedon looked around the overcrowded bar and tried to pick out bits and pieces of the loud chatter surrounding him. In one corner of the room, a balding toad of a man was trying to swindle land from a farmer after they'd drunk half a dozen drinks. In another, the notorious Madame spoke to a poor cobbler, no doubt attempting to recruit his daughter for her employ. With a slight swivel of his stool, Braedon also heard two off-duty knights discussing the growing group of raiders to the south. As he turned to listen further to the tavern's secrets, he received a hearty slap on the back.

The five fingers belonged to a foul-smelling heavyweight he called his friend.

Sir Don Falstone's breath smelled like he'd been drinking from the bottle. "My dear boy! I was just thinking about how I met you 10 years ago. That has to be at least 500 women ago."

Braedon smirked and looked the man over. While on first appearance it would seem as though Falstone had eaten more women than he'd bedded, the large, bearded man had his charms. There were few people who could hush a packed crowd with a simple half-true story the way Falstone could. Whether it was the adventurous tales or the family money that did it, he often left the bar with a girl on each arm.

Braedon remembered when he was wowed by it. He made no effort to replicate his friend's popularity, however, because he knew it was very likely to get back to his mother.

He took a sip of his ale. "And I'm sure you keep track of them all, Falstone, in a little black book."

The rotund knight clapped him on the shoulder and bellowed with laughter. Several others near the bar joined in his revelry.

"Five hundred is an estimate, of course. Besides, most nights I'm in no condition to be writing anything. Wouldn't want to accidentally sign away my inheritance to a girl I hardly knew." His fake teeth showed through his beard. "Sounds like something your father would do." Another laugh spread like wildfire.

Falstone always talked about Braedon's father. After the untimely death from a hunting accident, the portly noblemen said he would take the boy under his wing. Braedon's mother was less than pleased with the arrangement.

Since he'd come of age, Braedon had spent a fair amount of time among the heaviest drinkers in the land. As a result, he could tell he was the sharpest in the room, even with two drinks in his own system. He noticed an unmarked royal guard enter the building with an inconspicuous pouch.

Falstone's eyes grew wide. "Braedon, how long has your drink been empty?"

Braedon watched two more covert soldiers follow the man with the pouch. "And how long have you been as large as two men?"

The drunks beside them howled as Falstone put on a play frown for the crowd. The knight shook his cheeks as if trying to recover from a blow to the face. "It was long before your mother had to change your swaddling clothes three times a day. If my memory serves me correctly, that was just last week!"

The audience of their little exchange doubled over in laughter. Falstone gave Braedon a wink. Over his shoulder, the young man saw another two guards enter the room. They scanned their surroundings for danger before following in the direction their friends had gone.

Isn't this getting interesting…

Braedon contemplated what was in the pouch as he leaned toward the group of onlookers. "The only reason you know that is because you've been trying to catch a glimpse of me naked for years."

The men slammed their drinks onto the bar in delight. Two of them put their arms around Braedon as if they were best friends. In truth, he didn't know their names. He supposed there was no camaraderie quite so handsy as a bar friendship.

Falstone stood up to take back the attention. He grabbed a full mug from one of the men and tipped it toward his mouth. It took a few seconds, but he easily drank the entire thing. Then he tossed it behind him, where it expertly landed flipped onto its top. The happy mob cheered.

He wiped his mouth with his sleeve. "I think you had me mistaken all these years, my boy. See, the only one I wanted to see in the buff was your dear, sweet mother."

The walls of the tavern echoed with the loudest laughter and applause of the night. Braedon sensed the victory of the exchange had been awarded. He also watched as the final guard entered and snuck to the second floor.

That's a lot of guards for a little package.

Falstone walked over to his side and hugged Braedon with all his might. While the young man felt somewhat suffocated, he knew the rosy-cheeked idiot cared for him as much as any man. Maybe even as much as his father had.

"My friends, I watched this boy grow up from nothing, into…" The gaggle of drunks laughed in anticipation. "The fine young miscreant you see before you. When his father and I served in the war, who knew that I'd end up rich, and he'd end up bedding the finest woman in the land?"

Braedon glanced past the giggling rabble and through one of the windows to the outside. A blur went by for half a second. Nobody else would've caught it, but Braedon wasn't just anybody.

"And the inevitable result of that bedding sits before you on the prowl to bed someone himself."

The men slapped each other on the shoulder and took gulps from their beverages. Meanwhile, Braedon analyzed the direction of the blur in his mind. It was headed for the back of the building.

"So let's raise our glasses to Braedon!"

The gang called out his name and raised their glasses. Braedon did the same as he looked up toward the ceiling.

Falstone smiled like a proud father. "Here's to a new generation of bad behavior."

"Hear, hear!"

As the crowd drank, Braedon wondered if the guards knew they were being watched by two people that night.

He spoke in a soft tone that no one in the bar could hear. "Looks like this night could get exciting after all."

CHAPTER 4

Cinderella listened to the alcohol-infused laughter as she scaled the building unseen. Her fingers and feet easily found their grip along the side of the tavern. Unlike most missions the Godmother sent her on, this one gave her a hint of nervousness.

"You've retrieved plenty of items for her, Elle. This one is no different." Her boots found a resting spot beside the window to the second floor. She peered inside and watched a group of guards stand in their posts. Even without their official attire, she immediately recognized them as the queen's soldiers.

"Great. That's a nice detail you decided to leave out." She wiped the sweat from her palms onto her black cloak. "It's only 10 years of prison if I get caught. No pressure."

Cinderella had faced thousands of hours of training before her mentor let her go on her first mission at the age of 16. It was exhilarating to go from punching dummies made of straw to taking out abusive husbands. She'd personally foiled more than half a dozen assassination attempts by the seedy underbelly of the village. It was strange to be working against the royal family, but the Godmother had given Cinderella far too much for her to question her trainer's methods.

She took one last glance inside the window to plot her attack. As her mentor had taught, she pictured it all in her head with a long, deep breath. All the nervous energy she stored inside exited into the cold night air.

She smiled with confidence. "Showtime."

Cinderella patiently pulled open the window and slipped inside without the guards noticing. She tiptoed along what she assumed were creaky floorboards, though her agility kept any sounds from being made. There was just enough shadow for her to crouch in the corner and watch. The queen's men were in the middle of a long hallway. Two of them stood in front of a door that no doubt led to her objective. She spied another two milling about on the other side of the floor, and she had to figure there were at least a couple more in the room.

She saw a half-empty pint glass all the way at the other end of the hall. She dug into her pocket and pulled out a small stone.

Cinderella rolled the round projectile between her fingers. "Nothing gets the attention of men quite like spilled ale.

She wound up and threw the stone past the unsuspecting guards and directly into the side of the glass. The shattering sound was more than enough to get their attention.

As they both turned to mourn the tragedy, Cinderella snuck behind them and took two lightning-fast swipes with her sword. The blade cut through their scabbards, sending their weapons clattering to the ground."

When they jumped and faced her, she met their astonished looks with a smile. "Hello, boys."

They rushed her. The heavier of the two tripped over his own weapon and slammed on his elbows. As the other one bent over to grab his sword, Cinderella struck. First, she kicked him square in the top of the head. After he stumbled backward, she pursued, grabbing hold of either side of his head and wrenching him to the floor. His forehead met the wood and both cracked in response. He groaned as he tried to recover. The guard swung his sword so hard that when Cinderella avoided it with ease, the weapon stuck into the wall.

She laughed as he tried unsuccessfully to pull it free. "I guess you just don't know your own strength."

He left the blade in the wall and charged for her. With two swift movements, she punched him in the gut and elbowed him in the back of the neck. He joined his friend in the unconscious club on the ground.

Two additional guards came sprinting from the other end of the floor, their boots crushing the broken glass on their way toward her.

As they screamed and ran, she calculated. At just the right moment, she leapt high above their outstretched swords. Cinderella flipped once in midair and landed in a crouch behind them; before they had a chance to turn, she swept their legs out from under them. With two more kicks, she had their swords sliding across the floorboards until they hit the other end of the hall. When they attempted to rise, Cinderella slammed their heads into one another. They landed back on the ground with a thump.

She loved the feeling of her heart speeding up. "So far, so good."

Cinderella listened to the sounds of the remaining two guards readying themselves for an onslaught inside the room. She tried the room next door to them. Finding it empty, she thanked the stars above that she didn't break in on any extracurricular activities.

Cinderella shut the door gently behind her, walked to the wall furthest from the guard room, leaned on her right hand, and prepared her shoulder. "This is going to be either incredible or incredibly stupid."

She sprinted for the wall and crashed her shoulder through the paper-thin barrier. Her body cut through like it was butter. As parchment and wood broke apart in front of her, she saw the frightened guards standing by the door. Both of them dropped their swords and put their hands up.

One with the slightest hint of a mustache spoke with a quiver in his voice. "Just take it. It's in the drawer. Please don't hurt us."

Cinderella smirked beneath her mask. "Don't mind if I do."

She opened the drawer and placed the pouch in her pocket. With three swift strides across the room, she leapt over the bed and reached the window.

Cinderella opened it and took a step onto the ledge before turning back. "You two may want to punch each other and tell them I did it. Just a suggestion."

She heard the two guards scuffling as she pulled herself up to the roof.

Cinderella rolled out her shoulder and gathered herself in the darkness. She placed her hand inside her pocket and felt the jewel in her palm. It was warm.

"The queen and the Godmother both want it. It's gotta be a weapon, right?"

From the other side of the roof, a man cleared his throat. She let go of the jewel and placed her hand on the hilt of her sword.

"I hear thieves aren't well-tolerated in this kingdom."

Cinderella stood up straight and faced the man. Even in the nearly pitch black of the midnight sky, she was able to make out his features.

"Neither are drunks, from what I hear." She tightened her grip. "Begging your pardon, Prince Braedon."

CHAPTER 5

Cinderella watched the surprise spread across the face of the queen's son. She'd seen him paraded around the village in his youth, though his role in raising village support had diminished a bit in the last two years. From what she'd heard, he was getting support from the village the old-fashioned way.

The prince laughed. "You have good eyes, thief. It's a shame you didn't become a soldier."

His voice was kinder than his reputation, and his handsome face outdid both. She expected him to be skinny and sickly-looking, but he must've fit in some training between beers, because he packed a fair bit of muscle on his arms and his legs. Cinderella told herself she was only looking at his body to assess his weak points.

"Judging by the skill of the men I just defeated below, the training of a thief may suit me better."

He took a step toward her, and she inched the sword out of her scabbard.

Braedon put up his hands. "I don't have a weapon, aside from my charm, of course."

She scoffed and put her weapon back in the holster. "Aren't you just too predictable?"

The prince smiled, his teeth glowing white in the dark night. "I wish I could see under your mask. I want to know more about you."

Cinderella knew she had a little bit of time; after all, few soldiers had the agility to reach the rooftop. She wondered how long it would be before the bowmen assembled to try to flush her to ground level.

She took a step closer. "My apologies if I want to keep this conversation one-sided, but I have someplace to be."

"Please, you're already the most interesting person I've ever met. A lady thief who can easily take out half a dozen men. Hearing your story would surely beat the same old bar tales I'm always hearing."

She shook her head. "But how could I be more interesting than you, Prince? A man with all the choices in the world who opts to slum it in the village, hanging out with the seediest of characters, and bedding everyone who comes to mind. One might assume you're compensating for something."

He chuckled and lowered his stance. She wondered how long it would take to bring the court-trained fighter to his knees.

"You know, I may have you all figured out, too. You have all the telltale signs of a scorned orphan. Someone took you under their wing to train you, but you don't even know what you're fighting for." He bit his lip. "I'll bet you don't even know what's in that pouch."

Cinderella grumbled as she heard the footsteps of men coming toward the tavern. The steps were too well synced for them to be normal villagers. Reinforcements had arrived.

She sighed. "Oh, noble Prince. You have figured out everything about me, and now I will give up this life of crime and crawl into your bed." She matched her fighting stance to his. "Why don't we get this started, lover?"

He danced back and forth on his toes. "A fight on the first date. Doesn't seem like a good sign."

As he leaned forward, Cinderella whipped her back leg around and came within an inch of his face. When he ducked back, she came in low and cracked her fist into his chest. Before she could pull her arm back, the prince caught her wrist and twisted her arm against the joint.

He pressed her wrist toward her shoulder. "Nice technique."

She grunted and did a full backflip to get her arm going the right way again. As he marveled at her acrobatics, she broke the grip, took his own wrist, and secured it behind his back.

Cinderella pulled his arm against the socket. "I don't have to hurt you. Just stay down and look the other way."

The prince struggled to break free. "Why would we end the date so early?"

He loosened his shoulders just enough to worm his way out. But when he spun toward Cinderella, she met him with an incredibly fast succession of five punches. He blocked the first two, but the other three found their mark on both cheeks and right under his chin. As he staggered back, she almost felt bad for damaging such a pretty face. Almost.

Braedon rubbed at his jaw. "I can't tell if I'm in love or about to pass out."

Cinderella rolled her eyes. "I think I know which one."

As she went for the knockout blow, the prince easily sidestepped the punch. He caught her with two quick elbows and a jab to the midsection. Adrenaline coursed through her as she countered with three jabs of her own. One of the strikes found its mark so expertly, she could see the prince's eye begin to swell.

He continued to swagger as if he had the upper hand. "I truly am having a lot of fun."

"Are you sure that isn't the ale talking?"

"No, I'm not."

Cinderella smiled as Braedon came at her with a flurry of quick punches. She counted at least seven, and she feinted or ducked every single one. She came back with blows of her own, all of which connected with flesh and bone. As the prince started to lose his footing, she kicked him in the gut, sending his feet backward and his face to the floor.

He somehow groaned and laughed at the same time. "Best two out of three?"

She looked down to the front of the building, where the archers had assembled.

Cinderella admired the prince's stalling. She pulled his hair to get a look at his eyes. They were extremely blue and deeply inviting. She refused the invitation. "Don't follow me."

"Who are you?"

"Just a common thief." She winked, and then took a running dash toward the edge of the roof and leapt away onto the next building.

CHAPTER 6

Cinderella felt around in the dark of the creepy, old building where she'd spent so many of her midnights. Even though she'd passed so much time there that she could make it through most of the training area and the surrounding rooms by touch alone, she actually knew very little about the woman who'd pulled her out of the lowest point of her life.

Cinderella's fingers brushed one of the old practice dummies she'd spent years pounding upon. She felt the tattered stitches of the roughly woven face, remembering how often she'd pictured the inanimate opponent as her sister, as her stepmother, and as her father. She'd punched and punched until her knuckles were raw and bloody. On those nights, the Godmother had been the one to gently ease her hands away and into a bucket of ice.

Her hands could use the ice today after slamming so hard into the prince's bone and muscle. He was thicker than he looked, and one of the reasons she hated fighting drunks was that they needed an extra few punches to take them down.

This wasn't just any drunk, though. It was the Crown Prince of Loren, and he was standing between her and her mission.

Why'd you have me steal from the queen? What is this thing?

Cinderella's hand moved along the practice area and made contact with the weapon rack. She recalled the pride at mastering every one-handed, two-handed, and long-distance tool of war the Godmother possessed. Her late nights of training even included using random objects she might find along the way. She'd become so handy with a shovel, she sometimes preferred it to a halberd or mace.

Nowadays, she only practiced once or twice a week. The rest of the time was dedicated to missions that served some greater purpose.

Not that I'll ever know what that purpose is.

Her fingers traced along the wall just the right number of paces from the rack and found the lantern. As she illuminated the room, she was hardly surprised to see the stoic face of the Godmother staring right back at her. As usual, she seemed to materialize out of thin air.

The woman spoke as if she were holding something back. "Do you have it?"

Cinderella had never been able to determine her mentor's age. It was like she was preserved in the sweet spot of middle-age, and her face had barely acknowledged the passage of time in the decade they'd been training. Aside from a thin, gray line of hair down the side of her cheek, the woman seemed to have found the secret to defeat aging. It wouldn't be the only secret she'd kept from her protégé.

"Of course." Cinderella stretched her achy fist as she pulled out the pouch. "I think at this point I know better than to come back without completing a mission."

She pulled the stone out of the bag and felt it in her hand. It was even warmer than it had seemed before. The lantern made the red gem glisten. It wasn't the prettiest item she'd obtained for the Godmother, but it did seem to hold some kind of mysterious power. She could feel it in the way it seemed to change its temperature. She could feel it in the way the Godmother looked at it: with fear and hope in equal measure.

Her mentor gestured and Cinderella placed it in her hand. The Godmother turned the gem over with her fingers and held it up to her eye.

"You know, a little validation on this one would be nice. It wasn't the easiest thing to get."

The Godmother continued examining the stone. "Yes, I heard. Half the village is talking about a thief battling Prince Braedon on a rooftop. Your stealth is commendable."

Cinderella put her hands on her hips. "I could've ended it before any spectators started watching, but I didn't think you wanted any princes thrown off the roof."

Her mentor ignored her and walked swiftly to a desk where she began scribbling a note on a piece of parchment.

"Did you want princes thrown off rooftops?"

"No."

Cinderella snorted. "Good. I'm so glad we had this talk."

She began to walk away until the Godmother cleared her throat. "I need you to do one last thing today."

Her protégé stopped in her tracks and sighed. In the silence, Cinderella felt the bruise forming on her shoulder from her earlier effort to break through the wall. She waited for her mentor to finish the note.

The Godmother placed the gem back in its pouch and handed it and the parchment toward Cinderella. "I want you to give this to Tristan."

Cinderella raised an eyebrow. "So it's a weapon?"

"Of sorts."

She looked her mentor in the eye. "Is the reason I never get answers from you because you don't trust me?"

The Godmother walked back over to her desk and sat down. It was only after a few moments of quiet that she answered.

"You'll get answers when you're ready for them."

Cinderella picked at her nails. "I know you're not going to tell me, but I might as well ask why. I did take down six soldiers and a drunken prince. Not exactly a snatch and grab."

"If the queen truly knew what she had, she would've doubled the number of guards."

"That's comforting."

The Godmother sighed and pushed away from her desk. She slowly glided over and put her hand on Cinderella's shoulder. "Just take it to Tristan. I promise some things are about to become clear for the first time in your life."

Cinderella looked away. "Uh huh."

Her mentor reached for Cinderella's chin and pointed her face upward. "You did a good job tonight. Thank you."

Cinderella's heart fluttered with affirmation, as much as she didn't want to admit it. She nodded and tucked the items away.

She crept into her stepmother's home about an hour before dawn. She'd oiled every hinge and lock in the house monthly for the last decade. Between her stealth, the constant covering of Kiyara, and the non-creaky doors, Cinderella hadn't been caught on her nighttime jaunts for ages. As she lay down upon her stiff, unforgiving mattress, she thought about the red stone that was warm to the touch. She wondered if the Godmother was right. She wondered if she'd soon learn the answer to the greatest question of all.

CHAPTER 7

Prince Braedon woke up so sore he could barely sit up. As he stretched his arms skyward, he heard a pop in each of his vertebrae. Then he brought a hand up to his throbbing face. It was swollen and raw.

His cheek ached when he smiled. "She was something else."

The image of the thief standing upon the roof, a few stray strands of her golden hair blowing in the wind, consumed his thoughts. He never even saw her face. Her body was almost completely concealed in her fighting cloak. And yet, he didn't care whether or not he saw all the outward signs of beauty. His heart pumped a little faster for her.

A short healer entered the room with his head bowed, making him look almost dwarf-like. He recognized the man from some of his previous late-night encounters with a fist and a boot.

The dark-skinned islander looked up at Braedon's face and opened his eyes wide. "It looks like you were in battle."

The prince nodded. He'd love to share everything about the encounter, and about the incredible female thief, but he knew how fast rumor traveled. If Falstone found out the thief was a woman, the prince would never hear the end of it.

Braedon put on a brave face for the healer's stinging salve. "You should see the other guy."

The islander nodded as he dabbed the prince's eye. "People are saying that the thief fought dirty."

The prince's memory was immaculate after only three drinks, and there was no foul play whatsoever in his fight with the thief. But he knew the darkness of night could play tricks on the spectators below, and he wasn't about to dispel the rumors.

"The thief was fast, but definitely not interested in a fair fight."

The healer's eyes told the prince that this clarification of the rumor would make its way around the castle pretty quickly. There was only one person he hoped the news wouldn't make it to.

"Braedon!"

The healer rose and stood at full attention as the Queen of Loren stormed into the prince's room.

Braedon sighed. "Come to wish me well?"

If there was one word to describe his mother, it was proud. She stood tall and regal wherever she went. Falstone said he looked just like his mother, though he often prefaced it by saying he was an uglier version of her. They shared the same sandy-colored hair and blue eyes. They were both tall and had a much-stronger-than-average constitution.

But it was their pride that stood out among the other attributes. And her pride was never hurt more than when word spread about her son doing something stupid.

The queen waived the healer away, and the short man sprinted out the door.

She took over the islander's job and began dabbing additional salve on her son's wound. "More like I've come to finish you off."

His mother was much less gentle than the healer, and the prince squirmed in pain beneath her fingers.

"I'm not going to say it's any better when you get into a scuffle in some back alley. But at least then we can control the story better. Everybody saw you fighting, and they know she got away with whatever you were trying to protect."

Butterflies multiplied in the prince's stomach. "You heard it was a woman?"

The queen put on a sly smile and moved to the other side of his face. "I have better sources than your healer, Braedon. Don't worry, I've kept your reputation intact." Her grin spread. "Were you completely drunk or was she actually that good?"

The prince shifted to his side and stood up. "I think that's enough, Mother. My eye is bound to heal in the next few days."

"Fine. You don't have to tell me anything about the fight. But you'll need to speak with the Captain of the Guard about the thief. She stole something very valuable from the crown."

Braedon nodded. "Sure. But she didn't exactly tell me where she lived or anything."

"We'll make do with the info you give us." The queen took Braedon by one of the few unaffected parts of his face. "Why do you have to be so much like your father? He would always come back from the bar with a bruise or two. Even after he became king."

The prince knew he was a grown man, but he couldn't help but feel a bit soothed at his mother's touch. "Does that mean I have permission to rough it up at the tavern?"

She looked deep into his eyes. "I wouldn't go around following the lead of someone who died before his time."

Braedon had no idea what to say to that, and he sensed a quiet emptiness.

The queen stepped away and broke the silence by opening the curtains wide. The sun burned the prince's eyes more than any salve could.

"I'm worried about you, Braedon. If even half the rumors are true about how you spend your nights, then nobody will take you seriously when you become king."

There's that word again.

The prince groaned and turned away from the sunlight. "Can't you just live to 100 so I don't have to worry about that stuff?"

The queen laughed. "With soldiers retiring so fast, I'm lucky if I last the week."

Braedon had heard rumors, too. People had been saying that dozens of the queen's soldiers had either abandoned their posts or quit in the last month. In about half of those cases, the men left after experiencing a tragedy in their families. He wondered if the guards needed guards.

His mother interrupted his thoughts. "You know, that eye of yours should heal just in time for the midweek tea."

The prince ran a hand through his hair. "That's this week?"

"It's always been this week. It's an important event leading up to the ball."

Braedon wished he had a drink. *There's nothing he wanted to do* less then get dressed up and dance around with the prissiest women in the kingdom.

"Yes, Mother."

She stormed over from the window. "Don't 'yes, Mother' me, Braedon. You have certain responsibilities in this kingdom that I've let you dance around for years. But it was always leading up to this." She took his wrist. "You have to get married, have a child, and keep our lineage going. If you do nothing but these three things, then people will forget your misdeeds and think of you as a productive king."

"And what about love? You really think I'm going to find true love among these terrible women?"

His mother tightened her grip. "Not with that attitude you aren't."

He sighed and tried to roll out his wrist. His mother was stronger than she looked.

"I will try to keep an open mind. That's all I'm promising."

She gave her approval and let go. "Good. This afternoon I need you to help choose a new Captain of the Guard. Of course the old one retired, and we need someone to take his place."

The prince raised an eyebrow. "We should really look into these retirements, Mother. They have to be connected in some way."

The queen attempted to wave his thoughts away. "It's all about morale. We're working on it."

He shook his head. "No. I want to talk to the former captain."

"It's a dead end. He's lost all interest in the job."

Something about losing all interest reminded him of another rumor. The men who'd quit had lost all their passion. All their will to serve. There had to be something tying all of them together.

"You want me to be involved? I'm going to go investigate."

"Braedon, we have people for that."

The prince stepped up to his wardrobe and removed some clothes for the day. He couldn't remember the last time he went out when the sun still shined.

His eyes danced. "But why should we let them have all the fun?"

CHAPTER 8

Like on most days, Cinderella fought the urge to leave her stepmother's home and complete the task while the light still had a part of the day. Instead, in an ongoing mission the Godmother wouldn't let her quit, she pretended to be the weak little girl that Armenia ordered around from dawn until dusk.

At first light, she prepared breakfast for her four family members, not that she ever saw her father take a bite. After watching her stepsisters and Armenia eat like a ravenous pack of wolves, she washed the previous day's clothing by hand and then started the long list of tasks set out for her. As her hands kept busy, her mind processed the possibilities of the red gem hidden in her tiny bedroom.

She asked me to take it to Tristan, so we're going to use it to fight against something. But what?

"Did you hear me, peasant girl?"

Cinderella hid her ire and looked up from the chair she was polishing. Armenia loomed over her like a disapproving statue. Cinderella had actually liked her stepmother when she first met her. She was pretty and proud, and the young girl who'd just lost her mother thought this new woman could help her on the path to a happy childhood. But any smiles she'd seen before the marriage turned quickly to sneers and disapproving glances. Cinderella only saw Armenia laugh when it was at her stepdaughter's expense.

She produced a subservient smile. "Yes, Mother?"

Armenia gave her a glance that could kill. "I asked if you pressed our dresses for the tea this week. We can't have the prince seeing us look like common folk, now can we?"

While Cinderella kept the laugh to herself, she couldn't help but wonder if her rooftop encounter with Braedon had left him with any visual bruises. What excuses might he use to explain away the marks of her fists? Hunting accident? An errant slide down the golden staircase of the castle?

"I have, Mother."

Her stepmother stormed around the room like the queen she believed herself to be. "I'd like you to do it again. Stay up all night if you have to. These dresses must look perfect."

Cinderella nodded. "Of course. Would you like me to do it right now?"

Armenia beamed, clearly enjoying the feeling of total dominance. "You can finish in here first."

She walked out without a kind word or even an insult. She left with the same attention she might give a lame house pet or a stranger. Cinderella might have felt a new wave of pain with every uncaring exit if she hadn't hardened herself to handle the village at night. She wondered how many stepdaughters and partial orphans hadn't been so lucky. How much pain did they store in their hearts every single day?

With footsteps louder than a horse clomping through a city square, Malina appeared at the doorway. Like her sister, she was long-legged and beautiful, with soft skin. But the darkness inside of her honed her features to a sharp point. Her face at neutral looked more likely to cut a man than caress him.

"And while you're at it, Elle, can you take an iron to my undergarments as well?" She primped herself as if there were a mirror in the room. "I'm not sure if it will be the tea or the ball, but I have a feeling the prince is going to see more than my dress. If you know what I mean." She laughed her cute, irritating laugh.

Cinderella wanted to tell her stepsister that the best way to get the prince in bed was to put a keg in it, but she saved all the useful advice for Kiyara.

"I'll put it on the list, Sister."

Malina took long, exaggerated strides into the room. She leaned on the chair her stepsister polished. "What was it like?"

Cinderella had played this game before, though the rage remained difficult to keep at bay.

"I don't know what you mean."

Malina leaned forward like she was about to share a juicy piece of gossip. "What was it like to watch your mother burn to death?"

Cinderella's memory flashed back to the day it happened. She watched the red flames circle around her as her mother lay in the middle of it all. She closed off the memory before the tears could come.

When she stood up beside her stepsister, it wasn't the lowly cleaning girl in that room. It was the thief of the night, and Malina took a step back in fear.

Cinderella wanted to toss the entitled witch through the window, but she kept her attack to words only. "If you really wanted to know, a similar scenario could be arranged."

Malina hesitated before taking a speedy exit.

With a tension-releasing sigh, Cinderella closed her eyes. "I don't think I'll tell the Godmother about that."

When every light in the house had been extinguished, the thief took her cue to come out and play. Moving from shadow to shadow and flying through the air between rooftops made Cinderella feel free. She knew that one day she could let this sensation come out during the day, but that would have to wait until after the Godmother gave her permission.

Until then, she reveled in the crisp, dark air of the night.

She arrived at Tristan's house, which was situated in a sort of professional district of town. An expertly crafted metal sign in the shape of a hammer swung on a wire hook above her. She rapped on the door three times.

A small girl opened the door slowly. The child's red hair was partly matted from sleeping.

Cinderella laughed. "Now Hannah, aren't you supposed to be in bed?"

She suppressed a yawn. "I wanted to see if you were coming."

A wide man smelling of iron and flame placed his hand on his young daughter's shoulder. "She knows your knock, Elle. Come in."

Cinderella stepped into the modest blacksmith's home. A warm fire crackled from one side of the room, while the delicious smells from a plate of smoked meat and cheese wafted over from the other.

"Were you expecting me?"

Tristan's smile wasn't pretty, but it was so genuine that it lit up the room regardless. "I heard you embarrassed the prince on a rooftop last night. I thought you might save the victory tour for tonight."

Cinderella felt a tug at her cloak.

Hannah's eyes were like saucers. "Did you bring me anything?"

Her father gave a disapproving glance. "Honey, what did I tell you about begging?"

The little girl blinked her tiny eyelashes. "It was just a simple question."

Tristan sighed.

Cinderella looked between the two of them and felt the tug of a loving household. Her heart nearly opened up before she caught herself and closed things back off again.

"Close your eyes, first."

Hannah shut her eyes tight and put her small hands over her face. The thief produced a small candy from her pocket. The little girl opened her eyes and looked as though she'd just received the biggest surprise of her life.

Her expression was pleading. "Can I have it, Father?"

"Only if you get your little behind up to bed right now."

Hannah flashed a mischievous grin. "Thanks, Elle."

With that, she dashed up the stairs and disappeared.

Tristan shook his head. "That girl is going to be the end of me. I'm helpless against her."

"I don't think they make a weapon for that."

He sighed. "No. No, they don't. So, what do you have for me?"

Cinderella pulled out the pouch and removed the red gem. The way the blacksmith eyed the jewel made her wonder if she'd given two people candy that night. He reached out and she placed the stolen goods in his hand.

He looked stupefied. "It's warm."

She watched the candlelight flicker through it. "I know. What is it?"

Tristan turned the gem with his meaty fingers. "If the Godmother didn't tell you, I'm not sure I'm at liberty to say."

Frustration bubbled within her. This wasn't the first secret the Godmother had tried to keep from her. After all, she didn't even know the woman's name.

She gnawed at the inside of her mouth. "Just tell me something. I had to punch a prince in the mouth to get that."

"Don't act like you didn't enjoy it. Come with me."

They walked through the back door to the main smithy area. Weapons of all shapes and sizes lined the walls. She recognized many of them from the racks in the Godmother's secluded training facility. In the center of the room was the smelter and the rest of Tristan's equipment. Whenever he worked late at night, Cinderella would try to sneak a peek at the scaldingly hot room and watch the bulky man do what he was put on this earth to do. She imagined it was like watching performers act or dance, though she'd never seen such a thing herself.

Tristan set the jewel on a metal table he'd no doubt made.

He continued to look at the shining red object as if it were a birthday present. "It's ancient."

Silence stuck to the room like the black soot that clung to the walls.

Cinderella shrugged. "Okay. So it's old. Is it a weapon?"

"It's not a weapon, per se. But I think I know why she sent you here." Tristan met her eyes. "Something's coming, Elle. Something dangerous."

"What else is new? We can just stop it like always."

He lowered his voice, as if the windows had ears. "I've been hearing stories. Terrifying ones. Talks of men having the very lives sucked out of them. Their hearts turned black and leaving them a shell of what they once were."

Cinderella tapped her foot. "Uh-huh. Sounds like my father. It doesn't mean there's something evil. Some people just give up."

When Tristan tried to give her a sympathetic look, she simply turned away.

"What happened to your mother was a tragedy, Elle. That could destroy any man. But when it's a pattern...." He leaned in toward her. "I hear the Captain of the Guard just up and quit. He shut himself off from the world."

As a creature of the night, Cinderella had tussled with the captain before. He wasn't much of a challenge for her, but he also wasn't the kind of person who gave up. Maybe there was something to these rumors after all.

"And this gem is supposed to protect me?"

He smiled that broken, comforting smile. "It will when I'm through with it. Give me a day, but in the meantime be careful."

"I spend my whole life being careful."

The blacksmith's laugh was like a hammer hitting steel. "I think we have different definitions of careful. Maybe you'll understand when you have a family of your own."

Cinderella thought of her stepmother and the awful Malina.

"No thanks."

He smiled knowingly and patted her on the back. "It was nice seeing you, Elle. You have to come over for dinner sometime."

Both of them knew that would never happen given her situation, but it was nice of him to ask.

"I appreciate it." She took one last look at the gem on the table. "I think it's about time I paid a visit to our dear retired captain. There's nothing I love more than voluntarily visiting a man who wants me dead."

CHAPTER 9

Braedon walked into the tavern and was surprised to hear neither drunken revelry nor fighting. He tried to remember if there was a holiday as he took in the foul odor of spilled ale and sweat. The man behind the bar gave the prince a nod and gestured to the end of the room. Braedon spied a large, rotund man hunched over next to a half-filled glass. The flesh of his wide face pressed into the wood countertop before him.

The prince raised eyebrow at the barkeep. "How long has he been like this?"

"Not sure. Can't remember how old he is." The bartender winked and headed into the back room.

Braedon walked over to Falstone and shook the paunchy man by his shoulder.

With a deep breath of air, the unconscious drinker roared back to life. He immediately grabbed his mug and downed half the contents before noticing the prince.

His squishy face took on a stupid, happy appearance. His speech was slurred. "If it isn't the Crown Prince of Loren." He gestured to the room as if there were a crowd of hundreds. "Did you know this man before you is practically my son?" Falstone pulled Braedon in close. "I taught him everything I knew. And now he's all grown up. It's kind of tragic when you think about it."

Braedon wormed out from under the drunk's arm. "There's nobody here, you old fart."

If Falstone heard the prince, he certainly didn't understand him. "Did you hear me, everyone? I love him like a son."

The prince shook his head and took the seat next to his friend. He attempted to match the volume of Falstone's bellow. "I need to ask you a few questions."

Falstone appeared to comprehend him for a second, until he stood up and threw his arms into the air, sloshing his drink on to the prince's lap. The room-temperature ale soaked through his pants immediately.

"When his father died, everyone in the palace wanted to mourn and wear black, but I said no. That's no way to show a boy what's possible in life. So I took him on adventures."

"I should've come earlier." The prince looked toward the empty tables and chairs. "Before the show started."

Falstone continued to step forward. "And when he was old enough, most of the adventures happened right here."

Braedon grumbled. "I need your help, Falstone. Just let me know when you're ready."

"I remember... I remember when we slew a dragon together!"

"It was a dog. And we weren't slaying it. We were finding it because you lost it."

Falstone looked over at him. "I know the story." He blinked a few times. "Braedon, when did you get here?"

The prince let out half a sigh mixed with a laugh. "It doesn't matter. Can you tell me about the Captain of the Guard?"

The boisterous barfly wiped some of the spilled ale on his arm with his shirt and sat beside the prince. "Of course I can. He and I had a few adventures back in our youth as well."

Braedon rolled his eyes.

"Don't give me a look like that, Prince Grumpy. Me and the captain go way back. We fought in the war together. He was the only one who could drink me under the table."

"Did you hear about his wife?"

Falstone nodded. "A real shame. I was there the day he met her at the brothel. She was fiery."

The prince wondered how much truth his friend put into his elaborate stories.

"Does it make sense that he retired after she went missing?"

Falstone's face made its best drunken attempt at incredulous. "Not at all. He'd search for her to the ends of the earth, but from what I hear, he's holed up in his house. Won't even answer a knock at the door. It doesn't make any logical sense."

The prince tapped his fingers on the bar. "No, it doesn't make sense. It's like he changed into someone else."

Falstone looked deeply into Braedon's eyes. He leaned in as if he were about to speak great truth. "Braedon?"

"Yes?"

"Never change."

And with that, Falstone once again fell asleep on the counter.

The prince laughed to himself as the bartender came back into view.

"Get the old man some water, will you? If for nothing else than his awful breath."

The barkeep nodded.

Braedon wrung the ale from his pants. "I've got some work to do."

CHAPTER 10

As Cinderella snuck between buildings onto the street where the captain lived, she couldn't help but feel that someone was watching her. A glimpse of something out of the corner of her eye here, a far-off, faint noise barely within earshot there. There were few things she knew better than the sounds of the night.

Someone wants to play a game. Oh, we'll play a game.

The thief ducked through several alleyways, and when she reached a dead end she knew all too well about, she climbed up the side of the building and waited for her pursuer. As she gripped the stone with her dexterous fingers, she recognized the person behind her by both walk and smell. With the agility of an assassin, she pushed her feet off the wall and landed softly below.

"What are you doing here, Kiyara?"

Her meek, leggy stepsister turned with a jolt. Her face made it seem as though she had failed her objective. "I'm sorry, Elle. I couldn't sleep at the house, and I got tired of keeping watch for you."

Cinderella walked over and patted Kiyara's shoulder. "It's okay. But you might want to warm up your legs, because there's a slight chance we'll be running for our lives."

Kiyara almost smiled, which was like a win in itself. "Could be fun."

"It always is."

They walked and spoke in soft tones in the dark alleys of the village.

Cinderella mostly charted the next twist or turn, but she stole occasional glances at her silent sister. It hardly made sense that Kiyara and Malina came from the same awful woman. She'd overheard enough conversations to know that her stepsisters had been through a lot in their youth, but the two girls certainly handled their hardships in different ways. Kiyara looked as though she was always ready for the other shoe to drop. And Malina seemed to be the one holding all the shoes.

A light breeze cooled the long walk as the half-moon lit their way to the house owned by the former Captain of the Guard. As they approached the door, Kiyara froze before they could get close enough to knock.

Her look was uncertain. "Something about this place feels strangely familiar."

Cinderella eyed the house. Years ago, when she was in a particularly rebellious phase, she would leave notes telling the captain about fake heists and missions she planned to undertake. Few things made her laugh more than watching the massive, authoritative man wake his family and rush out in the middle of the night. One time, she laughed so loud from a nearby rooftop that the captain nearly spotted her.

This looked like a completely different house. It was somehow colder and darker, as if the life had been sapped from it.

The thief nodded. "Something about this place feels creepy."

She stepped forward and knocked on the door. It swung open from the rapping of her knuckles. A stale odor and unsettling darkness met them from the inside.

Cinderella could hear her sister's heartbeat pounding.

Kiyara cowered even further back. "Looks like nobody's home."

"Sadly, we can't give up that easily." The thief pressed the door open with a loud creak.

The light from the moon made the dark contents of the house look gray. Cinderella motioned to her sister and took several steps inside. Truth be told, it wasn't the first time she'd snuck into the captain's house, but things felt different back then. Even late at night, it had felt lived in. As if a child had grown up there. As if a family had been forged between these walls.

Now, it was as cold and lifeless as a crypt.

Kiyara stumbled into a chair, and a puff of dust wafted into the air. "I don't like this place, Elle. I think we should go."

"You should go."

Kiyara covered her mouth in shock as Cinderella followed the old, monotone voice back to its possessor. The Captain of the Guard looked leaner than the thief remembered. He shuffled toward them like a wraith. The moon only lightly highlighted his features, but it was enough for Cinderella to see his dim, soulless eyes.

The thief crossed her arms. "Is that any way to speak to an old friend?"

The captain lit a lantern, which added color to the room but not warmth.

He looked over toward Cinderella and betrayed the slightest hint of recognition. "I'm retired, thief. Play your games elsewhere."

She smiled. "I'd be happy to leave you alone until your funeral, where I assume I will be giving the eulogy. But first, I need some answers."

The captain was a stoic statue. "Just leave me be."

Cinderella was used to a little more back and forth between them, but she felt for a man who'd endured such tragedy.

"Where's your daughter? Is she staying with someone else since your wife disappeared?"

The man's eyes seemed fixed forward on nothing in particular. "I don't know."

His tone made Cinderella's adrenaline begin to bubble. She'd seen enough: a father who'd forgotten to care about his child.

"I remember you telling me you did everything for your daughter."

"Leave." There was no emotion in his words. "See yourself out."

As the man moved to turn around, Cinderella dashed like lightning to step into his path. "Your wife went missing, Captain. From what I've heard, you've done nothing about it. Were you the one who did it?"

His voice remained measured, which infuriated the thief even more.

"I don't know what happened to my wife, and I don't care. Leave."

Something broke in Cinderella as she slapped the retired soldier in the face. "You don't care? And your daughter might be out in the streets somewhere, and you don't care about her, either?"

The captain didn't react. Neither from the blow to the face, nor the impassioned questions. He was like Cinderella's father in every way.

"Leave or kill me. It doesn't matter."

She moved to slap the man again, but Kiyara took hold of her wrist. It was a stronger grip than the thief expected.

"It's not worth it, Elle. We should go."

The captain seemed to notice Kiyara for the first time. A hint of pain showed in his eyes, but it was gone as quickly as it came.

He stared directly into the stepsister's face. "I know you. You were here."

Kiyara took a step back. "I've– never been here before."

The wraith continued to fix his gaze. "You were here."

When Cinderella looked toward her sister, she saw something in the window. Actually, it was someone. The whites of the eavesdropper's eyes met hers, and he leapt away from the house.

"Stay nearby." The thief sprinted out the front door.

She turned to the side of the house and glimpsed the back of a leg running the opposite direction. Cinderella doubled her speed and ran toward the spy. She tried not to think about the strangely-altered captain.

Despite her best efforts, she couldn't help but connect the dead eyes of her former adversary with the vacant glare of her formerly loving father.

Cinderella reached the back of house, only to see that the eavesdropper had hopped onto a building on the other side of the cobblestone street. She heard a late-night carriage in the distance.

"He's fast."

She reached deep into her reserves and pulled out a little more speed as she followed the path left by the man at the window. As she tried to scale the same building he had, once again, she only saw the slightest part of him reach the roof. Cinderella listened to his footsteps slapping against the top of the building, and she stretched for the next handhold. Her fingers slipped at the same time one of her feet gave way. The thief's stomach lurched as her remaining hand on the building carried her entire body weight.

"Damn!"

A familiar wave of anxiety came over her and her instincts kicked in. She swung herself off the exterior with her remaining hand and flew toward the ground. Her reflexes sharpened to a point as she approached the unforgiving stone below. Cinderella tucked her head and rolled at just the right moment. What could've been broken bones or a shattered spine for the untrained was nothing but a light and perfect impact on her rounded back. As she completed her tumble and looked up, she saw the eavesdropper's gaze following her. He ran out of sight before she could identify him.

She grunted in frustration. "Godmother isn't gonna be happy about this."

Cinderella heard a little girl's scream back in the direction of the captain's house. She took one second to release a loud crack from her spine and ran toward the noise. Behind her former rival's home, and far across the street from Cinderella, she saw Kiyara standing a few feet from the captain's daughter.

The little girl pointed at the stepsister and screamed her words in a high-pitched voice. "You did this to my father! You made him hate me!"

Cinderella couldn't hear her sister over the calamitous sound of the approaching carriage on the road, but Kiyara's face was red and splotchy. She was crying, and it wasn't pretty. Cinderella waited for the carriage to cross, but as she did, the captain's daughter took off running. The little girl tripped and fell face forward in front of the quintet of horses bearing down on her. Cinderella's heart skipped several beats when she knew she'd never reach her in time.

PART 2

CHAPTER 11

Prince Braedon's chest heaved as he tried to catch his breath. He bent at the waist and thanked his lucky stars that he hadn't gotten a drink with Falstone before his little one-on-one race with the thief.

His words came out in sharp bursts. "She's really fast. Strong and fast. It's almost unfair."

He could barely hear himself over the clattering hooves of an approaching carriage. From his perch on the rooftop, the prince heard a little girl scream. Instinct worked better than his lungs as he scaled down the building with relative ease. Braedon saw a young woman crying as a girl who couldn't be older than ten seemed to scold her with an accusatory finger. He saw the carriage in the distance, just as he noticed the little girl's hips were pointed to the street.

His eyes widened. "Not good."

Several steps into his sprint, he noticed the thief to his right. There wasn't enough time to stop and protect himself. He blocked everything out of his mind and channeled all his energy into the muscles of his legs. He watched the girl begin to run toward the loud and unforgiving danger that came for her.

Braedon whizzed by the thief and saw the girl trip into the middle of the road. His lungs burned as he bent down at full speed and hoisted her off the stones and out of the way of the lead horse. He was surprised by how far he was able to throw the child just as one of the legs of the carriage animals slammed hard into his knee. He felt his body twist in ways it wasn't meant for, and the pain was an excruciating knife up his side. The horse knocked him clear of the carriage, but the damage was already done. Attempting to put weight on the injured leg nearly sent him to the ground in agony.

Through watery eyes, he looked into the little girl's face. Her fear told him she was far from safety.

She reached for him. "Help me!"

Ignoring his pain, he took the girl's hand and limped toward the nearest alley. There wasn't enough time to identify the young woman, but her sobs echoed through the village. The little girl cut off the circulation in his hand with her iron grip as they went as fast as they could between the two buildings. With every step he took on the injured leg, a blinding wave of fire pierced his every sensation. The tiny fingers wrapped with his were the only thing that kept him conscious.

The girl directed him through the darkness. "She didn't look like that, but I could recognize her eyes. I'll never forget those eyes."

The prince didn't have the wherewithal to respond, but he knew that the shadow of the thief couldn't be far behind. He'd sprinted in hundreds of foot races on the grounds of the castle, but he'd never felt his heart beat this fast before.

He wondered if he'd ever race again.

The girl led him to what looked like a dead end, but there was a small hole in the corner of one alley wall, just big enough for her to fit inside. She tried to pull him through the small opening, but he squeezed her hand to stop her.

"I'll hold them off. Get as far away from here as you can."

The girl nodded and let go, and soon she disappeared into the darkness beyond.

Braedon heard the sound of clattering footsteps behind him. This was not the noise a thief would make if she were going for the element of surprise. He knew she could smell the blood in the water.

Braedon looked around for something to defend himself with and came upon half of a broken axle in the alley.

He gingerly bent down with one leg and lifted the piece of wood into the air. The leg with the twisted knee barely felt like it was part of his body anymore. It hung there, useless, and continued to send him signals of overwhelming pain. "Really feeling like a pirate here. Just gotta replace the broken knee with a peg."

Through all the agony and the fear, he hoped that joke wouldn't be his last. The footsteps came to a stop, and the thief walked out of the shadows.

Her eyes looked concerned. "Is she okay?"

His voice sounded more frantic than he wanted. "Why? You only like to hunt them when they're healthy?"

The thief removed the cloak from her face. A small part of him hoped she'd be ugly or homely. Instead, her full lips and light blue eyes made her stunning in the moonlight. It was like she was from a dream, but if she slit his throat, he figured it would be a little more like a nightmare.

She spoke softly. "I'm not hunting her."

The prince attempted to laugh, but it came out more like a wheeze. "The girl said your friend was chasing her or something. Whatever you're doing, it sure doesn't sound harmless."

The beautiful woman before him took out a knife and tossed it onto the ground. It sparked as it skidded across the stone.

"We're on the same team, Braedon. She's the captain's daughter and I have no intention of hurting her."

From his time at court, the prince had heard an incredible amount of lying and untruth. That's what made honesty stick out so much more.

He dropped his makeshift weapon. "Thank the gods."

As the adrenaline dissipated, his awareness of the pain doubled in an instant. His vision went from blurry to black, and he felt his good leg start to give out. He thought he heard the thief call out his name just as the dark filled everything.

CHAPTER 12

It didn't take Cinderella long to find the girl. She was cowering in the corner of an abandoned home, and once the thief disarmed the captain's daughter of the piece of glass she brandished, the little lady collapsed into her arms.

In her years working for the Godmother, Cinderella had learned where all the queen's soldiers lived. She left the girl on the doorstep of the army's second-in-command, waiting just long enough to make sure she was inside before dashing off. She rushed back to make sure the prince was still where she left him. Sure enough, he remained unconscious but breathing.

Fortunately, the Godmother's place was only a few streets away. And while the prince was heavy, he wasn't even close to the heaviest man she'd ever carried.

To distract herself from his weight, she tried to put some of the puzzle pieces together. "How did the girl know Kiyara? The captain knew her, too. She hardly even leaves the house without being under her mother's thumb. It doesn't make any sense."

She looked down at the unconscious in her arms. "And how did he get so damn fast? If he'd been that quick on the rooftop, then it would've been at least a little tougher to punch him in the face."

Cinderella took the bruising on the side of Braedon's cheek as a sort of trophy.

"Never injured a prince before."

He murmured in his unconsciousness.

"But I'm not against doing it again."

It felt like ages before she reached the Godmother's home, and laid the prince down just inside the front door. As she sat and rested off the exhausting walk, Braedon awoke and clutched at his knee.

"Do you have a healer?"

Cinderella scoffed. "Sure. I think he comes in about a half-hour after the massages, and the live-in musician."

He tried to smile. "The girl's safe?"

Cinderella nodded.

With pain covering his face, he moved himself into a sitting position against the wall. "Good. I think I've done my good deed for a lifetime, then. Where are we?"

"If I told you about this place, I'd have to kill you."

The prince grinned and grimaced. "Sounds nice." He looked straight into her eyes. "Seems like as good a place as any for our second date."

He saved a little girl. Do not punch him in the nose.

Cinderella stood up and paced around. She could feel Braedon's gaze upon her.

"You know, I've seen so many women who are full of themselves in court, but you're the only one I've met who is truly confident in herself."

She sighed. "Uh-huh."

Cinderella wished the Godmother would just show up already. Then she could figure out what exactly happened to the captain. She could also get away from the eyes that followed her every move.

"How does one get to be that sure of oneself? Lots of stolen jewels?"

She glared at him. "More like dozens of slain princes." She put her hand to her chin as if she were in deep thought. "Where should I bury the body this time? The north bank of the river is particularly nice for corpses, but the catacombs might be a better fit. Such difficult decisions to make."

Braedon laughed uncomfortably. "You're kidding." A few beats of silence went by. "You are kidding, right?"

"She's kidding."

They both looked over to see the Godmother gracefully walking in with a medical bag of some kind. Nothing ever seemed to faze the woman, and now she could add broken-kneed prince to the list of situations she could easily handle.

Without introducing herself, Cinderella's mentor began rolling up Braedon's pants leg. He squirmed from the pain, and the Godmother quietly shushed him. She looked over the injury with gentle, soft hands and nodded to herself. The way she inspected the leg with such care was mesmerizing.

"Lay him down somewhere with light so I can get a better look."

"Carrying him all the way here wasn't enough?"

The Godmother returned an irritated glance that compelled Cinderella to take action.

She hoisted the prince up with ease.

His eyes widened. "You carried me here? What are you, three quarters goddess, one quarter elephant?"

"Call me part elephant again, and I might have to drop you on your head."

The prince kept his lips sealed as she moved him to a better location. She once again tried to ignore his constant stare. As soon as he was lying below the lantern, she turned and walked to the far end of the room.

The Godmother removed some sort of bandage from her bag and began wrapping it around the prince's knee. "I know she won't say it, but saving that girl and putting yourself at risk was very brave."

"How'd you know… thank you."

Cinderella piped up. "I was getting around to saying something. Just trying to get over his loathsome personality first."

Braedon gripped the ground beneath him as the Godmother tightened the bandage. "She's just mad I was faster than her."

"Oh, I know. I've learned all her tics by now."

Cinderella snorted. "I don't have tics. Besides, this isn't a friendly conversation. It's an interrogation. What were you doing listening at the captain's window?"

The prince flexed and unflexed his wrapped leg. "A guy can't just go around saving little girls and call it a night?"

When nobody laughed, he gulped a bit. "Tough crowd. I have a feeling I was doing the same thing you were. The captain isn't the first soldier to start acting… strangely. Dozens have had something horrible happen to them and then they decided to retire. But maybe that's because this one is threatening to slit their throats."

The Godmother rested her hands on her hips and trained her eyes on her protégé. "You threatened the captain?"

Cinderella seethed. "This is why I don't like eavesdroppers. Yes, I exchanged a few harsh words with him, but it was because he didn't even care about his missing wife and his devastated daughter. He'd just given up."

"The wife is dead. Her body just washed up in the river today."

Cinderella folded her arms and looked away. "Damn." She sighed. "I kind of liked her."

The prince leaned up on his elbows. "I don't think he did it."

"No." Cinderella chewed on her cheek. "He wouldn't have done that. But I also thought he wouldn't give up hope, and I was wrong there."

The Godmother looked up. "There's something deeper going on here. Few things are ever what they seem on the surface."

"And like always, I'm the one who has to figure it out."

The prince smirked. "Is she always this moody?"

"She's usually worse."

Cinderella threw up her hands. "You two are terrible. Feel free to solve the case on your own. I'm out."

With that, she stormed outside before the others could say a word. The cold breeze of the night sent a chill through her. She wrapped her arms around herself and leaned back against the wall. She took deep breaths to slow her adrenaline.

It didn't take long for the Godmother to come out. She wore the smile of someone who had been through it all and made it to the other side. Her mentor put her hand on Cinderella's shoulder. It lingered there for several moments.

"I'm sorry this reminds you of your father."

The thief looked to the stars. "It's not fair. Losing someone is bad enough, but when the people left don't care anymore... it's pure torture. And now I'm supposed to help the captain? Who, I might add, never liked me much in the first place."

The Godmother rubbed the side of Cinderella's neck. "Don't think about helping him. Think about that little girl. If you can give her the peace that you never had, wouldn't it be worth it?"

She felt her chest open up. "You're very manipulative. You know that right?"

"I do."

"Let me sleep on it." Cinderella looked back to the front door. "You'll keep him safe?"

Her mentor's mouth curled into a smile. "Are you asking because you care about him?"

Cinderella rubbed at the goose pimples that formed on her arm. "Of course not. He just saved someone's life. I think that earns him a free pass for the next 24 hours or so."

As the Godmother continued to smile, Cinderella grunted and walked off as the pitch black of night started to give way to dawn.

CHAPTER 13

Cinderella hadn't realized just how long it took her to carry the prince to safety, and as a result, she reached her stepmother's house later than usual. After scaling the side of the house, she could hear Armenia calling to her from the hallway. She stripped off her functional thieving clothes and changed back into the drab garb of a servant girl. Seeing the transformation from feared criminal of the night to forgettable maid in the mirror never failed to take her energy down about a dozen notches.

"Coming, Mother."

"You'd better be, because the day just started and you're already far behind."

It had been about four years since Cinderella first asked her mentor if she could kill her stepmother. She waited until she had a foolproof plan to present, with at least a dozen reasons why it would be beneficial to the village. After all, it wasn't as if she was the only person Armenia belittled throughout her day. The Godmother rejected the plan, and the 13 subsequent spins on an assassination Cinderella presented later. It wasn't until last year that she stopped asking altogether.

"Yes, Mother."

She closed her eyes and unpacked herself. Cinderella left the nighttime warrior behind and stepped out into the hallway as a meek mouse who was ready to serve.

Not only was Armenia standing there with fire in her eyes, but the woman's wicked daughter was also beside her like a younger, angrier twin.

Malina sneered. "We know what you did last night. We know you weren't in your room."

Cinderella wished she didn't have to play this part. "I'm sorry."

Her stepsister lurched forward as if she meant to get physical, but Armenia held her back.

"Tut-tut, daughter. Wouldn't want you to accidentally bruise before the tea. I'll make sure your sister is handled correctly."

Malina gritted her teeth but took a step back. For the first time, Cinderella noticed her other sister was hiding at the far end of the hall. The thief by night still had no idea how Kiyara factored into all of this. She wondered how difficult it would be to get answers out of her reticent sister.

Armenia lifted her chin. "My ugly little worm of an unwanted daughter, I know that you didn't just leave the grounds without permission. You encouraged my sweet, innocent flower to follow along with you."

I wonder how innocent she really is.

"Yes, Mother."

Her stepmother strode forward and took hold of Cinderella's cheek like she owned it. "There are dangerous people in the village at night. I don't expect you to be smart enough to know that."

There was a time when Armenia's words were the most painful weapons against her, but that time had long passed. Her armor was strong enough now.

Cinderella tried to nod, but her stepmother kept her face locked in position.

"When was the last time you washed the linens?"

The thief kept her eyes cold and dead, no matter how much she wanted to reveal her true fiery nature. "Two weeks ago. It took several days."

"I think it's time for a little freshening. Do them all again today, in addition to your regular chores."

Armenia was asking the impossible. It was torture not responding how she really felt.

"Yes, Mother. I'm sorry."

Malina had such a large smile on her face, Cinderella bet she could knock out half her teeth with one well-struck blow.

"You should make better choices, sister." Malina glanced back at the shrinking violet that was Kiyara. "And you should know better than to hang out with the swine." She stomped away in a manner that could hardly be called ladylike.

Armenia maintained control over Cinderella's face. "I don't have to worry about you causing trouble this week, do I? As you know, the next few days could change everything."

It would be so easy to snap her neck right now.

"I know how important it is. You don't have to worry."

Her stepmother finally let go and disappeared into her room without another word.

Cinderella had become an expert at letting the rage seep out of her in the quiet moments of the day. As she let the hidden anger and pain subside, Kiyara walked into the light.

Her sister looked at her own feet. "This is all my fault."

The thief removed her veil of subservience. "She's done and said worse. I'll be fine." She tucked a strand of blonde hair behind Kiyara's ear. "But you need to tell me if there's something going on. I want to be able to help."

Kiyara kept from looking Cinderella straight on. "I don't know why the captain and his daughter recognized me. Sure, his house looked familiar, but Mother has taken us to lots of houses owned by important people in the village."

The thief knew Kiyara wasn't telling the full truth, but she wasn't quite up for using all of her interrogation techniques to get to the bottom of things.

"Okay. But if you remember anything, you'll definitely tell me?"

Her stepsister nodded without looking up, and walked away. Cinderella watched her as she went.

Why is she lying to me?

Before she could even fathom an answer, she heard a noise from behind the door that never opened. The shuffling of feet moved across the room. As much as she didn't want to listen, she stood there petrified. The man who used to play with her and hug her and love her still lived and breathed behind that door. Armenia never mentioned him, and her stepsisters must've been given some kind of warning to do the same. It was as if he never existed, but Cinderella's memories weren't lies.

"Did something do this to you? Or did you and the captain both just forget how to love?"

The movement on the other side of the door failed to answer the question as Cinderella stood there wishing she had the same ability to go numb and forget.

CHAPTER 14

Prince Braedon woke up free of pain. Without having to work a hangover out of his system, he actually felt better than he had in months. He looked down at his leg and flexed his wrapped knee. Aside from a little tightness, everything appeared to be in working order. He breathed in the perfume-free air of the village. He much preferred it to the overly sanitized ambience of the castle. It was like the air was freer out here.

"Looks like that healed nicely."

Braedon's body jumped from the shock of noticing the Godmother sitting in the darkness on the other side of the room. As his heart settled, he considered how many more secrets and surprises the strange woman had left.

He showed her his pain-free leg. "There's no way the healers at the castle could've fixed this so quickly. It's unbelievable."

"When you get to my age, you realize that pretty much anything can happen."

The prince shrugged. "I guess. I still can hardly believe how skilled our mutual friend is. I've been training at the castle from the age of four, and she beat me like I was nothing."

The Godmother moved to the corner of the bed and slowly sat. "Whether or not she knows it, Cinderella fights with the passion of her dead mother."

"Cinderella." He let the name sink into his every thought. "So she lost someone. I knew it!" As soon as he said it, he felt sheepish. "I'm sorry. I just get comfort out of understanding people."

"You can analyze someone correctly, but that doesn't mean you understand everything."

"I've lost a parent, too. People just deal with it in different ways."

A loud noise resembling a wild animal clomping into the house stole their attention. The sound of several items being knocked over preceded Falstone poking his head in through the door.

His eyes were red and bleary. "Braedon! I've been looking all over the place for you." He glanced over to the Godmother sitting on the bed. "Oh man! I hope I didn't interrupt morning cuddle time."

The prince was mortified as the turned toward the Godmother. "I'm so sorry. I don't know how he found me."

Falstone barged his way in. "I've got eyes and ears everywhere, my boy. Never knew you were getting experience from an older woman in the bedroom."

While Braedon's cheeks turned red, he was surprised by just how calm the Godmother was at his drunken friend's presence.

She stood up. "You must be Falstone. The rumors of your personality hardly do you justice."

Falstone nearly tripped over himself to kiss her hand. "My lady. Don't believe everything the boy tells you, for he tends to exaggerate. Same with the rumors. Basically, don't trust anything you ever hear about me."

The Godmother relinquished her hand. "I'll keep an open mind."

Falstone crashed down on the bed next to the prince, sending the aroma of sweat and pure alcohol into Braedon's face.

"By the gods, Falstone. Where did you even come from?"

His friend ignored the question and spoke in a very audible whisper. "You've got to tell me all the details. I never knew you had a thing for silver, if you know what I mean."

The prince's neck felt hot. "Just tell me why you were looking for me."

Remembering himself, Falstone dug deep into a pocket and pulled out a piece of parchment. "A messenger came wandering into the tavern this morning. I thought it was better if I delivered it. It's always best to hear news from a friend."

"Fine. I just think that protocol should be amended to include that friend taking a bath first."

"It's from your mother. The Queen of Loren!"

Falstone cleared his throat. Then, he raised his voice an octave in an effort to impersonate Braedon's mother. "Braedon. I don't know exactly which alley you slept in last night, but it would behoove you to return home this instant for the planned tea with the ladies of the kingdom tomorrow. I hope that you will think of your mother when you make your next set of decisions."

The prince put up his hand. "Please, Falstone. Stop making that voice."

Even the Godmother seemed to crack a smile at the impersonation.

Falstone stood up taller and puffed out his chest. "You don't believe my portrayal is accurate, dear Prince? Why, I could walk right into the castle today and take over. I just need a wig and some makeup."

"And a shave. And a diet to lose about... 200 pounds?"

Falstone wrinkled his nose and tossed the parchment onto the bed. "I was just trying to have a little fun, my boy. You should remember fun. In fact, I had a lot of fun the last time I had tea. I was put in a precarious position where I had to choose among three women to invite to a tea my father was holding. So, naturally, I brought all three and–"

Now the prince cleared his throat. "That's enough, Falstone. The lady and myself have no interest in hearing this."

"I completely understand. You want to save the naughty stories for behind closed doors."

The prince wasn't sure his face could get any hotter. "Falstone, I will see you later today."

The old drunk scratched at his beard. "I once took some time to learn from the older generation. I was with the woman who was maybe two... no, three years my senior–"

Braedon hopped off the bed and pushed Falstone through the open door until the large man had cleared the threshold. "Goodbye."

With that, he shut the door firmly.

Falstone spoke through the wood. "I'll save a seat for you at the tavern."

The Knight of Ale clomped his way out of the building.

"You keep very interesting company, Your Highness." The Godmother stood up.

The prince attempted to breathe out the embarrassment. "Falstone has really been there for me. At a time when no one understood how much pain I was going through, he was the only one who made me feel normal again."

The Godmother nodded. "I understand. I just wonder if you've gone long enough dulling your senses."

Braedon raised an eyebrow. "What should I do instead?"

"Come with me. I'll show you something that might serve as a viable alternative."

The Godmother opened the door and gestured for the prince to follow. To his surprise, he didn't even hobble out of the bedroom.

CHAPTER 15

The heat from the walls stung Cinderella's cheeks. Smoke burned her eyes as she tried to look around for the one reason she hadn't run away. The fire was so blindingly bright around her that she wasn't sure she could keep her eyes open that much longer. But she had to look. She had to find her amid the accumulating rubble of a collapsing building.

Her heartbeat quickened as she searched every last spot that had yet to be touched by the fiery killing machine before her. Her hands were slick with sweat as she cupped them to her mouth.

"Mother?"

Cinderella awoke with a start. Her face was pressed against the cold stone of the wall. She was surrounded by linens she'd spent the entire day cleaning. Cinderella rubbed at her eyes. "I'm glad the old witch didn't see me. Who knows what she would have done to me in my sleep."

She looked down at her hands. They were calloused and strong, but they weren't burnt. She had scars from that fateful night on her lower back, but her hands had somehow escaped without a lasting reminder. She sighed and returned to work for the remaining few hours until nightfall.

The thief arrived at the Godmother's house under the cover of darkness. Between thoughts of dirty linens and wanting to mount Armenia's head on a pike, she thought of Prince Braedon. Most of those thoughts revolved around how annoying and insolent he'd been over the time she had known him. Like most royalty, he usually seemed to think he was better than everybody else around him... but not always. After all, he had saved a little girl from dying.

I would never tell him, but that was pretty impressive.

Cinderella's thoughts were interrupted by a faint clanging sound behind her. She drew the sword from her scabbard and turned toward the noise. As she crouched into a fighting position, a burst of air sprung up behind her and she felt a light slap on the back of her head. As she turned to swipe at the blur, her blade struck nothing but air.

She grunted as she rubbed at her hair with her free hand. "Show yourself."

Another noise prompted her to step forward. The second she did, another burst of air zipped through the room and she was struck in the same exact spot, this time with a fist. For the second time, she was too slow to get a weapon on the attacker, her sword frustratingly hitting nothing at all.

Cinderella's instinct was to get angry and swipe her sword in every direction. Instead, she thought through the many lessons the Godmother had given her. She withdrew her weapon and closed her eyes. A whole new world opened up to her, with her other four senses focused in response. She controlled her breath and waited for something to happen. When the next speedy attack came, the thief used her training to duck down and sweep her leg at just the right moment.

With a yelp of surprise, a man whose voice she recognized tumbled to the ground. Cinderella opened her eyes to see Prince Braedon dusting himself off.

Cinderella smirked. "I see the knee is feeling better."

He sprung up into a crouched position. "It might be better than ever after what the Godmother taught me. You up for another round of sparring?"

"You call that sparring?"

The prince grinned and made a run at the thief. Sure, he was fast, but things were a little easier when she could see him coming. When he got close enough, she slipped underneath his left arm, hooked under the armpit, and used his own momentum to toss him halfway across the room. He landed on his upper back with a satisfying fall. The heir to the throne of Loren groaned in the dust.

Cinderella cracked her neck to one side. "The element of surprise works much better for you. I'd stick with that." She looked up through the window. "Besides, I was planning to spend my time patrolling for whatever it was that killed the captain's wife.

The prince was up quicker than she expected. "You need to take me with you. This is the most fun I've had in ages."

"Fun? You were nearly killed by a raging carriage. You call that fun?"

The prince relaxed his face. "I know that you would. Why should I be any different?"

While the Godmother didn't seem to be in the room, Cinderella could feel her presence throughout. She knew what course of action her mentor would take.

The thief and the Prince patrolled along rooftop after rooftop, looking for anything out of the ordinary in the sleeping village. Cinderella attempted to adjust her typical routine to include a sidekick, but said royal sidekick seemed to want nothing more than to start a conversation.

The prince remained slightly out of breath the entire time. "So, the Godmother told me your name. Would you rather go by Cindy? Ella? Inder?"

Every time the prince attempted to speak, Cinderella sprinted away from him and leapt to the next rooftop. The prince followed, never getting quite as much distance as she did in her leaps.

"I just don't wanna keep saying 'hey' and 'you' instead of addressing you by your preferred name."

Another run and another leap away from conversation.

The prince was relentless. "You know what, I hear that we have something in common."

Cinderella could feel her blood starting to boil. "If you say a dead parent, I'm going to twist more than your knee."

The prince's mouth gaped open in fake surprise. "She speaks! I guess you only do that when someone touches a nerve, Cindy?"

"Elle. Call me Elle. Let's just leave it at that."

Tonight's patrol had even less intrigue than usual. Often, Cinderella would find a knifing to stop or a trio of drunkards stripping off their clothes in a very public place. She wondered if the talkative prince was scaring off both the weirdos and the genuine leads.

She sat down and wrapped her arms around her knees. "We can take a break."

Braedon sighed with relief. "Thank the gods." He let himself slump down to a lying position. "I don't know how you do this every night. I could really use a drink."

Cinderella shook her head. "Sadly, Your Highness, they don't have kegs that run a line up to the rooftops in your noble village."

The prince lazily rolled over to her side. "It is sad. Speaking of sad, how did your mother die?"

Do not throw him off the rooftop. Do not throw him off the rooftop.

She shot him a death-glance. "Is this legitimate third date conversation?"

He smiled. "So, you're finally admitting that we've been going on dates?"

She looked away from him. "I don't want to talk about it."

The prince nodded. "Understood. My father died in a grizzly hunting accident. I never even got to see him before he passed away."

"I think I heard about that. You know, because your father was the king of this freaking country."

The prince sat up. "All I'm saying is that we have something in common."

Cinderella leaned away from him. She knew the Godmother would say that talking things out was always more helpful than keeping them in. But she spent all day doing things she was supposed to do, and frankly, she was a little tired of it.

"I can think of one small difference."

"What's that?"

Cinderella stood and walked to the edge of the roof. "You have a mother who invites you to tea. I have a father who hasn't spoken to me in years."

The prince joined her by the edge. "I'm forced to go to tea. It's different from an invitation. You would understand if you didn't have control–"

"Sssh."

Cinderella saw something familiar fluttering in the air. A small golden light danced across her field of vision. It was some kind of bird... an incredible, glittering bird. And the amazing creature brought back something from Cinderella's memories. She couldn't grasp exactly where she'd seen the shining animal before, but the golden shimmer was as clear in her mind as if she'd seen it yesterday.

"Did you see that?"

The prince blinked. "I saw something for a second, but I thought it was just a star."

Cinderella followed the bright golden bird as it fluttered down past the rooftops and perched in front of a house she recognized. It only waited for a second before it flew off out of sight.

"We're near the captain's house."

The prince glanced around. "Wow. Didn't we start here tonight? Think we've gone in a circle for the entire village."

Cinderella eyed the outer wall of the building next door. "I want to check it out again."

With expert agility, Cinderella pushed off the rooftop and aimed for the side of the other building. The second she came into contact with it, she pushed off the wall with her opposite foot. She repeated the same motion several times over until she'd rebounded off each building three times and landed softly on the ground below. She looked up at the bewildered prince.

"I think I'll just climb down. Meet you over there?"

Cinderella tsked and walked across the road to the captain's front door. She went to the exact location where the golden bird had perched. She placed her fingers on the spot, as if trying to conjure the memory where she'd seen the bird before. Closing her eyes and concentrating hard on her breathing, she couldn't come up with anything relevant.

The prince startled her out of her thoughts. "Now that's interesting."

Cinderella turned toward him. "What?"

He stepped forward and placed his hand on hers. A small bolt of nervousness went through the thief's arm and into the rest of her body. Her instinct said to withdraw her hand immediately, but she let her hand linger under the prince's touch.

Damn it.

The prince gripped her hand in his and pulled it off the front of the captain's house. Her eyes widened.

"Are those...?"

The prince nodded. "Claw marks."

Sure enough, something with sharp, powerful nails had clawed up the front facade.

Cinderella had seen a variety of claw marks and paw prints in her missions through neighboring forests, but these marks were larger than any she'd ever seen. Her blood pressure began to rise.

Prince Braedon seemed to be having the same reaction, as his face whitened. "What could've done that?"

Cinderella examined the door from top to bottom and opened it a crack. She shook her head. "I don't know, but there's a matching pair on the other side."

CHAPTER 16

Kiyara learned a long time ago not to ask her mother questions. When Armenia told her to put on something dark and leave the house in the middle of the night, she did it without a moment's hesitation. Her mother hadn't brought up the previous night's adventure whatsoever. It was as if she didn't even consider Kiyara had a part in it at all. All the blame was laid at the feet of Cinderella.

It isn't fair. It's never fair.

Kiyara thanked the gods that neither her mother nor her sister checked Cinderella's bed before they left the house. She prayed that none of them would see the thief of the night as they walked from their carriage to an unfamiliar part of town.

Her fears were never realized. They didn't see a single soul on the way to a house that didn't ring a bell in her recollection. The house was modest but well decorated on the outside. Kiyara stood behind her mother and her sister, playing with the fabric of her dress. "What are we doing here?"

Malina turned back with a sneer. "What do you think we're doing, genius?" Kiyara took a step back, which startled both a rat and herself.

Armenia clicked her tongue. "Sisters should support one another, Malina. You know that Kiyara has developed a unique gift of blocking out the past. Apologize."

Malina wrinkled her nose. "I'm sorry. Now can we get on with this?"

Armenia grinned with pride. She reached her hand toward the door and touched the knocker. Then her hand pushed through the door like it was made of nothing. The lock on the front had fully disintegrated before Kiyara's eyes. Her left arm began to twitch.

"I think it's time to pay our new friends a visit." Armenia gripped the new hole in the door and easily pulled it open into the street. Malina practically dove inside, while Kiyara required a bit of coaxing from her mother. The butterflies in her stomach were multiplying with every second and, with great hesitation, she stepped inside the unfamiliar house.

When Armenia closed the door behind them, it was nearly pitch black inside the stranger's foyer. Kiyara felt the tears begin to form in her eyes. "Can someone please tell me what we're doing here?"

Armenia sighed and snapped her finger. A lantern on the far end of the room lit up like magic. "We're just paying someone a little visit."

The ability to see everything around her failed to lessen Kiyara's nerves. "Then why did we break in?" The sound of a large man stumbling out of bed made the tears flow down Kiyara's face. She did her best to blend into the wall.

Kiyara spied the man of the household stepping into the light at the top of the stairs. She recognized the head bowman of the Queen's Guard almost immediately. Kiyara had seen him at various upper-class gatherings and parties. But she'd never seen him draw his signature weapon, which was pointed right at her mother's head.

The bowman pulled the string back a little tighter. "Who are you? And what are you doing in my house?"

Before he had a chance to react, a little boy ran between his legs and took the stairs downstairs.

"Son, no!"

But it was too late. The young child giggled as he watched the three women before him. Malina opened her arms wide and gestured for the boy to come close. The child was so fast, the soldier had no chance to turn his weapon on Kiyara's sister before she held the boy high in the air and between her and the weapon.

She laughed as much as the boy did. "What a beautiful son you have."

The bowman breathed heavily. "If you touch a single hair on his head–"

Armenia let out a deep, throaty chuckle. "Your little toy won't hurt her. You're out of your depth, bowman."

With that, the queen's best shot zipped a warning arrow to the side of Malina's head. It whizzed past her ear and lodged itself in the wall with a thud.

Kiyara bent to one knee and felt the bile moving up her throat. She started to dry heave.

Armenia faked a yawn. "You've revealed your weapon, and now it's time for me to show you mine." With one swift motion, Armenia closed the gap between herself and her daughter and touched Malina's shoulder.

Still gripping the young boy, Malina let her cloak fall to the ground. Then she looked up to the ceiling and opened her mouth wide. The alabaster skin on her arms started to change color as she expanded wider and taller. Her shoulders broadened and the soft delicate skin turned thick and scaled. Kiyara couldn't turn away from the sight that both horrified her and struck her memory.

I've seen this all before.

The bowman backed away from the edge of the staircase with horror. Once standing just above 5 feet tall, the grotesque demon had gained two full feet in height and its arms and legs were thicker than that of a horse. Fangs extended from her mouth and she let out a terrifying smile, as she pulled the bowman's son tighter.

"Father!"

The bowman didn't hesitate any longer. He fired an arrow directly for the chest of the beast Malina had become. With a wave of her hand, Armenia shot out a small ball of fire directly into the path of the arrow. The wooden shaft disintegrated before their eyes as the metal arrowhead lost its trajectory and clinked harmlessly to the ground.

Armenia turned toward Kiyara and raised an eyebrow. "It's time, my daughter."

Kiyara shook her head and started to back her way to the front door. Malina let out a floor-rattling growl, and Kiyara started to become lightheaded from fear. She kept backing up and backing up until she was pressed firmly against the door they'd originally entered.

As the bowman readied another arrow, Armenia turned and sent a fireball right into the man's prized weapon. The bowman screamed as his hands caught fire. He dropped the now-useless device.

Armenia turned her attention back to her daughter. "No more time for games." She took Kiyara by the throat and lifted her high into the air.

Immediately, the change began to take place on the inside and outside of her body. Pain exploded through every muscle from top to bottom.

Everything in Kiyara's body broke down and came back together again completely different. Her skin changed from white and soft to grey and stone-like. All her fear and pain began to slip away. Her mother released her grip and began ascending the staircase, where the bowman was calling out for his son in vain. Kiyara's hands grew long, wide, and clawed. She wished she could run away from herself as her mind went blank and blood-red with rage.

CHAPTER 17

The walls of fire once again warmed Cinderella as she walked through the flames of her dreams. In most of her dreams, everything she saw was hazy, but now things were starting to clear up. The edges had become less fuzzy and sharper around her. She saw the body of her mother laid out before her, and she wished that the woman she loved had her face turned toward her. She placed her hand, the hand of a child, into her mother's palm and squeezed.

The pain was ever present, though it was a distant pain.

As the flames began to inch toward her, she saw a familiar sight: the golden bird once again danced before her eyes. The shining light of its wings somehow stood out against the fiery red that surrounded her. The bird appeared to be trying to draw her attention. Was the bird actually gesturing to her? Was it leading her from the flames?

As Cinderella reached out to touch the bird and let go of her mother's hand, she awoke.

Cinderella needed a minute to decompress. It's not every day that the traumatic puzzle of her dream received a new addition. This was the first night of over a thousand that placed a golden bird at the scene of her tragedy.

Between a possible figment of her imagination and the claw marks that connected a series of crimes to her meek sister, Cinderella's week was getting pretty interesting.

With Armenia and her stepsisters heading to the royal tea, she had all day to try to work out the mysteries in her life. She started with several hours of training. First, a series of body weight exercises, which had long ago become far too easy without only using one hand or arm. Next, she put her body through a test of the fastest martial arts her legs and wrists could muster. It wasn't until she sweated out the fire from her dreams that she felt like herself again.

After bathing and taking a trip into the village, she thought about how much her life would have been different if the fire had never taken place. She knew that all of the strength and speed she'd gained over the years would be nothing but a dream. She'd likely be weak and whiny, headed to the tea herself. She'd be decked out in a frilly gown, giggling at the sight of Prince Braedon up close. She wouldn't realize how much he hated every moment of it. Maybe deep down, she would've hated it, too.

She sighed. It was no use to think of things that would never be.

After trading in her typical blacks for a garb that would blend in with the rest of the villagers in the afternoon, Cinderella didn't have to go far before she heard of the latest attack. Her heart sank when she saw the crowd gathered around another tragic late-night event. On one side of the enraptured mob, the fat knight known to be the prince's best friend jabbered away about the victim.

"Of course I heard the scream. You could've heard it down the entire street. If I weren't having a nightmare myself at the time, I probably would've run over and gotten myself killed from bravery. It was an awful, awful thing. The smell of fire was everywhere. A lesser man might have fainted from the fear."

Cinderella slipped deeper into the crowd, wondering if she could learn anything valuable from the large crowd's ramblings.

"Between the Captain of the Guard and the best shot in the land, I think that someone is targeting the bravest men among us. For all we know, I will be next. If the queen fails to give me half a dozen men stationed at my door at all times, I may just have to move to the next kingdom over. I hear Martone is lovely this time of year."

Cinderella resisted the urge to punch Braedon's buddy in the face. She stuck around with the rest of the murmuring crowd until the bulk of the queen's men had ceased their investigation of the bowman's house. Without the cover of darkness, she used her stealth and speed alone to sneak through an open window and into the site of the attack.

Cinderella crouched in the corner and waited for the last royal soldier to leave and close the door behind him. Her line of work had taken her to many tragic locations before, and they all had a coldness to them. They all felt as though something that made them alive before had been wrenched from their very being. Any of these locations, no matter how vibrant and alive before, reminded Cinderella of a graveyard.

She treaded lightly to avoid making a noise that would alert the soldiers outside. Now that she was looking for them, it was easy to spot the claw marks upon the front door. They were just as deep and unidentifiable as the ones from the previous night. She ran her fingers along the deep crevices.

"I really don't want to have to fight whatever made these marks." She looked around the room, but even in the day it seemed to have all the color pulled from it. "Knowing my life, I'll probably have to battle a dozen." She continued to scan the scene, spying an arrow that had lodged itself in the wall. From the trajectory and the angle of the projectile, she traced the possible origin back to the top of the stairs. She nearly tripped over a warped and burned weapon that lay in a pile of ash by the top step. She worked the ash between her fingers and examined its pattern.

"He was famous for this weapon. He wouldn't have let it sit in a fire. After he shot it, someone did something to him. But it doesn't make any sense."

She took another lap around the room to gather all the data she could. While she was able to ascertain that the creature with massive claws and who was able to somehow control fire had taken the bowman's child, it did not get her any closer to identifying who, or what, these things were. As she prepared to slip back through the window, something metallic caught her eye from between two floorboards.

Cinderella crouched toward the shining object and took a small chain in her fingers. She lifted it up off the ground and grasped it in the palm of her hand.

"Hey, you! What are you doing in here?"

The thief didn't have to think twice before taking three large bounds across the room and jumping through the open window. She put her hand through the loop in the chain and let it roll down until it was around her shoulder. She easily climbed to the rooftop before any other soldiers saw her and leapt across two additional buildings until she was far away. There, she let her heart settle.

"I like the darkness better."

She let the chain roll back down to her hand, and she spun it around to see what lay at the end. It was a fairly impressive blue stone that no doubt had come from somewhere far away and mystical. The light seemed to swirl about it like a low-hanging cloud. But Cinderella didn't need to take a second glance to know exactly whom it belonged to. She'd seen it around the neck of her stepsister Kiyara ever since the first day she walked into her life.

CHAPTER 18

The Prince breathed in the cold air from the high ledge outside his room. He looked down at the preparations for his impending tea; the early afternoon sun made everything below look disarmingly bright and merry.

"What a mirage. Perhaps the only cheery ones are the mothers forcing their sons and daughters to take action."

He bounced on his toes from side to side and considered scaling the three stories it would take to get up on the roof and hide from it all. Once in solitude, he might be able to finally understand the claw marks on the captain's door. Two sets of claw marks. Could a pair of hellish creatures be scaring the very soul and duty out of his kingdom?

"Fear and pain can do things to a person."

He could have pictured the Captain of the Guard or too many other soldiers who recently retired after making that statement, but the person he thought of was none other than Cinderella. He pictured the thief moving from rooftop to rooftop with ease. She was completely open to risking her life and limb for her mentor, but she was almost completely closed off to companionship.

He'd asked around about her mother's death, and it was particularly gruesome. The father, an earl, had withdrawn much like the soldiers of the past few months. What Cinderella hadn't mentioned was the demanding stepmother Armenia who had taken over her mother's position and life. It was no wonder the beautiful, blonde creature of the night had sunk into the darkness.

He was thinking about the moment when their hands had met when he heard a familiar voice calling from his open window.

"Your Highness?" Braedon's personal servant called out to the ledge like it was every day a prince would be hanging on the edge of death. "The guests are beginning to arrive. Your mother has put me in charge of getting you presentable."

The prince looked up. "It would be so easy to just hide on the roof."

"Prince Braedon? Your mother may have my head if you don't make it to the tea soon."

The prince nodded and glanced one more time at the roof before swinging his way into the room.

Braedon's mouth hurt from smiling so much, and his mind ached from the fakeness of it all. He nodded lethargically as a woman droned on about her teenage daughter who cowered beside her. The woman was incredibly hopeful, but her high-pitched wail of a voice led to the serious possibility of making Braedon's ears fall off.

"You can probably tell this by looking at her, but she is both smart and funny in equal measure. I feel like the luckiest mother in the world to be able to laugh and think so much in my own household. Of course, if a charming man like yourself happened to take her off my hands, I would mourn her absence, but who in their right mind would stand in the way of true love?"

One look at the young teen told the prince that she wanted to disappear from the entire conversation.

"There are so many beautiful women here, but let's face it, many of them have loved before. Nobody wants to be second best or second choice, right? With a young girl like my Mona, that's something you won't have to worry about. Would you be willing to take five minutes just to get to know her?"

Before the prince could answer, the queen graciously interrupted the exchange and pulled him over to another pairing of a mother and a daughter. Unlike in the previous sales pitch, this daughter appeared to be much more age-appropriate.

The ruler of Loren whispered in his ear. "Are you having a good time?"

The prince rolled his eyes. "I'd rather be stabbed in the eyeballs. But, I suppose it could be worse. I could be naked, running over hot coals.

"Please, leave your snark out of this. This could be a fine pairing for you." The prince put on his game face and examined the girl in question.

There was no denying her beauty. Her flawless skin and long, flowing blonde hair were very attractive. She had brown eyes and an ample bosom no doubt enhanced by the green dress she wore. Truth be told, the mother did not look much older than her daughter.

The queen gestured to the two women. "Prince Braedon, let me introduce you to the Lady Armenia, and her daughter Malina."

The prince hid his recognition of the name and reputation of Cinderella's stepmother. This was a woman who had tortured his sparring partner for over a decade. Her fake smile was even more plastered-on than usual.

"Charmed to meet you, too." He started by kissing the mother's hand before moving on to the daughter's. "I hope you're enjoying your tea. It's a little fruity for my taste, but my mother knew that it would be mostly beautiful women in attendance."

Malina leaned her chest toward Braedon. "It's not the kind of tea for a rugged man like yourself, my Prince."

Is she being serious right now?

The prince put on his most polite face as his mother's eyes widened.

Malina placed her arm on the prince's shoulder. She had a smile that seemed to indicate a desire to go upstairs. "Forgive me, Your Highness, but I've never seen someone so handsome up close. I absolutely had to touch you to make sure that you were real."

Even Armenia seemed a bit taken aback by her daughter's direct approach. "My apologies for my daughter. She's been kept so chaste and innocent for so long that she has no idea what to do when something like love comes over."

The queen smiled. "I completely understand. Love is a very strange beast."

Armenia wrapped her fingers around the prince's bicep. "It's pretty obvious you don't spend all of your time at court, Prince Braedon."

The prince wasn't sure how to extricate himself from the situation. He froze his face like a happy statue in response. "Thank you so much. I try to remain active."

Armenia placed her hand on the queen's back. "If you don't mind, I'd love to discuss a few matters of state while our children have a private chat."

Braedon attempted not to be sickened by Armenia's smile. He hoped his mother could sense the woman's evil through her tainted smile.

"But of course. Braedon, play nice."

Braedon nodded, a sculpture hiding his true feelings.

As soon as their mothers stepped out of earshot, Malina produced a small flask from her bosom. She unscrewed the cap and took a swig.

The prince chuckled. "Too much for you, as well?"

Malina wiped her lips with her arm. "It's a lot of pressure." She shook the flask from side to side. "I've almost downed the entire thing, but you're welcome to a swig. I've heard you're a fan of the drink."

The prince knew there were too many eyes upon him to partake. Besides, he'd actually been sober the last two days, and it left him feeling energetic.

He put up his hand. "Thank you, but you seem to be enjoying it far too much for yourself."

Malina tucked the flask back into its hiding place and put her arm around the prince's neck, pulling herself closer to him. "Let's get down to business, Braedon. There are a lot of girls here, but I'm a woman. I'm happy to fulfill all of your–"

"Who's that?"

The prince spied a lady his age sitting on the edge of a garden bench. She was shivering.

Malina tried to turn the prince away from the petrified attendee. "She's nobody. She happens to be my sister and I can tell you that she is little more than a cold fish."

The prince gently removed Malina's arm from his shoulder. "I think I'm going to give the cold fish a little company. I'll speak with you later, Malina."

As he walked away from her, he heard a frustrated, high-pitched yip from the inebriated damsel. He smiled to himself.

Armenia's other daughter continued to look away from him, even when he sat down beside her on the bench.

He gladly let the fake smile evaporate from his face. "Are you okay?"

His words startled the girl, and she appeared to shrink into herself as she turned around. "Oh. It's you. Yes, I'm fine."

"You don't look fine. You're shivering on a warm summer's day. That doesn't seem normal."

The girl let out a sad laugh. "I guess you don't know me very well. I'm not sure if I know myself well."

The prince scooted closer. "You're Kiyara, right? Cinderella's stepsister?"

Kiyara looked surprised. "I don't think my mother would be very happy to hear that you know about Cinderella. She wants Cinderella to be the girl that everyone forgot."

The prince marveled at how different Kiyara was from either of her sisters. She wasn't headstrong and tough like Cinderella, and she lacked the brash overconfidence of Malina. Of all the girls he'd met at the tea so far, Kiyara was certainly the most relatable.

He put his arm around her shoulder and she leaned into him like a little child. "I'm sorry for the other night. It was brave of you to save that little girl."

"That was you. You are the friend. I didn't put two and two together."

He glanced up and saw Malina giving him an evil glare from across the garden. He wondered if Kiyara's other sister would have any feelings about him having his arm around the fearful girl.

Kiyara nodded. "It was me. If it weren't for you, who knows what would have happened? Who knows what is happening...?"

The prince raised an eyebrow. "Do you know something about what happened to the captain?"

Kiyara sniffled. "I don't, but I have a terrible feeling about all of it."

The prince had a strange feeling of wanting to wrap a blanket around the depressed girl and protect her. "I feel the same way."

Braedon noticed a messenger walking across the grass toward them. He wore a somber look upon his face. The prince released his hold of Kiyara.

"More bad news?"

The messenger let out a heavy sigh. "I'm afraid so, Your Highness. There's been another attack. The head bowman's son is missing. You told me to let you know if any–"

The prince stood up. "I need to go. I need to put an end to this."

Kiyara looked up into his eyes as if she had something to say. Instead, she nodded and crumpled back down in her original, solitary position on the bench. Both the queen and Armenia stomped over toward him.

His mother spoke up first. "What exactly is going on here? What news do you bring?"

The prince stepped in front of the messenger. "Don't trouble yourself with it. It's something I need to look into, and the rest of you should enjoy the party. I'm sure you'll enjoy it more than I would have anyway."

Armenia did not appear to appreciate the comment. "But you'll return, right?"

The prince shook his head. "I'm sorry. I'm sure I'll see you and your daughters at the ball."

He tried not to look the queen in the eyes, but he knew the anger she felt for him right then. He knew he might be making a wrong decision, but he walked toward the stables anyway.

With all hands on deck for the tea, the prince was alone in the stables as he prepared his ride. He wondered whether staying in the village for another night would've prevented whatever it was cutting their army down one by one. He'd saddled his horse and was ready to hop up when he heard a noise behind him. He turned around in a fighting stance, only to see Armenia standing there in the stall. With the look she had on her face, Braedon wasn't sure it was smart to relax out of his pose of readiness.

He held his breath. "Armenia, you shouldn't be in here. You might sully your dress."

Her eyes were locked on his. "You had my Kiyara in your arms, and now you're stepping away as if nothing happened." She took a menacing step forward. "This is very distressing for me as a mother."

"I've never been one. I wouldn't know."

Her gaze was so focused, the prince wanted to turn away but couldn't. "You think you can do whatever you want, just because you have the backing of the crown behind you. You don't care what people get hurt along the way, do you?"

The prince gulped. "You're not the first person who's told me I should be more grateful."

Armenia took two more steps toward him. "I'm not saying you should be more grateful. I'm saying you should be afraid."

"Afraid?"

She stopped about a foot away from his face. "One day you're on top, but the next it can all come crashing down. And then, you'll do anything you can to protect your loved ones. Anything."

The prince nodded. "I understand." He did not understand.

"Today I have to leave for an important kingdom matter, but I promise you that I will have a dance with both Malina and Kiyara at the ball."

After another second of an intense stare, Armenia let her face soften into a smile. "That's all a mother can ask for. Take care, Prince."

Braedon did not hesitate. He jumped upon his horse, turned it around, and rode straight out of the stable without another word.

What in the heck was that?

As his horse trotted out the stable doors, Prince Braedon noticed a smoking trail of scorched grass.

CHAPTER 19

The light of the moon illuminated the small blue charm that Cinderella held between her fingers. She rubbed the pendant as if it would reveal its secrets to her. As she continued to touch her stepsister's necklace, she racked her brain to determine some kind of connection between the recent incidents and Kiyara.

Cinderella walked down a dark alleyway in the space between the bowman's and the captain's homes. "The most likely thing is coincidence. Kiyara dropped her necklace the night she was in the city, the beast somehow got it caught on its feet, and it dragged the charm inside."

Her mind recoiled a bit at her reflex to hide the truth from herself. "Perhaps, the creature was in Armenia's house. It could have rummaged through Kiyara's things in an effort to find something in particular. Maybe an object they had brought from whatever land they came from."

She reached the end of the street and looked both ways for her next direction. She wandered to the right. "Of course, the explanation that makes both the least sense and the most sense is that Kiyara has something directly to do with this creature." She sighed. "Her charm was at the bowman's house. The captain and his daughter both recognized her eyes. She was involved, but I thought she was the only one I could trust."

In the many years Cinderella had been tortured by the cruelty of her stepmother, Kiyara was the only one who seemed to care. With her father having gone into whatever dark hole his mind fell into, Kiyara was the only family she had left. Now whatever this situation was, whatever was taking the soldiers of Loren from their queen, might be taking the only family she loved from her as well.

She glanced upon the bowman's house from afar. There'd been no activity there since the previous night, and the guards had been doubled since she was spotted snooping around on the inside. Cinderella turned the other direction and continued walking until she heard a light wisp of the wind. It was just out of place enough for her to know what was coming.

"The Godmother must've shown you a nice trick or two the other day."

Two footfalls landed in front of the thief, and Prince Braedon stepped into the light. His blue eyes stood out in the moonlight. "I'm amazed you even heard me. I thought I was completely silent."

"You would think that, wouldn't you? You learned from the Godmother for a day. I studied for a decade."

The prince attempted to make himself look taller. "I am a fast learner."

Cinderella laughed on the inside. "You just keep telling yourself that." She stuffed the necklace in her pocket. She wasn't ready to share this clue with anyone but the Godmother. "How was the tea? Do you feel sufficiently wooed that you no longer need to fish for compliments?"

He gave Cinderella a strange look she didn't recognize. Could it have been fear?

"Your stepmother is a piece of work. If I didn't promise your sisters a dance at the ball, I think she would've strangled me to death."

Cinderella didn't know whether to laugh, add another reason to her laundry list of why the Godmother should let her kill Armenia, or some combination of both.

"Welcome to my family. I'm sure you didn't get the worst of it."

"Thank the gods for that." He glanced in the direction of the bowman's house. "Did you see anything interesting in there?"

Kiyara's charm burned in her pocket as she walked in the opposite direction. Braedon kept the pace with her.

"More claw marks. A lot of pain. A clue that doesn't make any sense."

She wasn't sure if it was her tone of voice, but she was glad the prince didn't push her further on the clue.

He shook his head. "I don't feel prepared for this, Elle. If this thing had us cornered, I don't know how we would stop it. After all, we don't even have an idea as to what it is."

"A friend of mine was working on a new weapon. Maybe it's exactly what we need to protect ourselves."

The prince shrugged. "Sounds like it's worth a shot."

Cinderella felt a little strange that the prince was entering every part of her life. He'd been to the Godmother's lair, and now he would meet one of her only friends in the world. It was an odd, slightly comforting feeling.

She shook it off. "Come with me."

As they took a rooftop path across the village to Tristan the blacksmith's home, the prince regaled the thief with stories from the tea. Instead of rebuffing him as she had before, she actually listened and asked questions in response. Since the silence made her think of Kiyara and whatever involvement she had in all of this, the absence of silence was actually somewhat pleasant.

Cinderella's hair whipped in the wind as they landed in sync on another roof. "We're close by. So, you're saying Malina made a pass at you?"

The prince grinned through heavy gulps of air. "Let's just say she undressed me with her eyes, and if I'd let things go further, she probably would have undressed me with her hands."

Cinderella shook her head and gestured toward another rooftop. The prince nodded and they leapt through the air one more time. There was something about tumbling through the air with another person. It felt right.

This time, she landed about half a beat before him. "Gods. Part of me can't believe she did that with so many people around. But the other part of me wonders if she would've taken things further."

The prince raised an eyebrow. "Further?"

"Something along the lines of stripping all her clothes off in the middle of the Royal Garden."

The prince's cheeks reddened. "While she seems kind of horrible, I might not have minded that so much."

She slapped Braedon in the shoulder. "Now that is gross. You are... just as disgusting as I thought you were the first time I met you."

He put up his hands. "Hey! I think I've earned a few points by now."

Cinderella rolled her eyes. "Now that we're on our fourth date, you mean?"

"You're the one who's keeping track, not me."

She laughed, and she didn't want to stop. Cinderella breathed the giddiness out. "You're terrible. The blacksmith's place is just below."

"I mean, I thought it was our second or third date at most."

"I should've thrown you off the tavern rooftop on day one. One should always go with one's instincts."

She didn't wait for his reaction as she began to climb down the building.

As they reached the ground below, Cinderella felt something in the air.

"You never would have thrown me off a roof. I would have stopped you."

Cinderella put up a finger and silenced him. The smell of the smoke reached her nose, and butterflies began to dance around her stomach.

"Something isn't right here." She slowly stalked toward Tristan's front door.

"Are you sure that isn't just the smell of the smithy? Maybe he's working on the weapon right now."

She shook her head. As the sign of the hammer came into view, she could see the blacksmith's front door very clearly. Her heart sank. It was black and burnt to a crisp.

CHAPTER 20

Cinderella's lowered shoulder broke through the charred door with ease. As she stepped into the once-familiar home, she could tell that nothing was as it should be. The furniture and walls and art she remembered from many trips inside had all been burnt in some kind of controlled flame. Her pulse raced as her eyes darted from side to side.

"Tristan? Hannah?"

She heard nothing in response.

The prince's eyes widened as he pointed to the side of the door. She saw what caught his eye.

He shook his head. "Claw marks. We're too late."

The sound of a man screaming filled the home. Cinderella recognized the voice immediately.

She ran up the blackened stairs as quickly as she could. "Tristan!"

As she came upon another locked door, her adrenaline reached the boiling point. With one firm kick, the door collapsed in on itself and fell inside. Smoke filled the room, though it was starting to exit through an open window. Cinderella covered her eyes and coughed. "Tristan?"

She heard a steady breathing inside the bedroom. She waved away as much smoke as she could, attempting to see through it.

She had to see if one of the only people she cared about was still alive.

The prince helped to clear the smoke out of the room with a quilt he'd found downstairs. Before long, enough of the gray cloud had cleared to reveal the blacksmith staring straight ahead. All the joy and fire that had occupied his eyes for as long as Cinderella had known him was completely absent.

She bit her lip. "Tristan?" She rushed to him and grabbed his arm. She felt a pulse, but she didn't know if there was anything left inside. "Please, don't do this to me. Tristan?"

The blacksmith didn't even acknowledge her presence. He continued to look straight ahead, as if nothing could revive him from his stupor.

She pounded at his shoulder. "Look at me, Tristan. Where is Hannah?"

Nothing. He had nothing left.

The prince tried to take Cinderella by the arm, but she violently shook him off.

"Tristan! You have to tell me where your daughter is, or she might die."

He didn't move. He didn't care.

Cinderella placed her hands on the front of her forehead and screamed. She'd started to pull at her hair before the prince finally got her attention.

"There's no time for that, Elle. The only way to save his daughter is to find her. You need to keep it together."

Cinderella wanted to take Braedon by his throat and slam him into the wall, but she balled her hands into fists and restrained herself. "Okay." She tensed and untensed her fingers. "Okay."

As they stepped toward the door, Tristan opened his mouth. "Workroom."

Cinderella dashed toward him and looked into his eyes. That one word was all that had been left in him. Now there truly was nothing.

She sighed heavily. "We'll find her. I promise you."

He said nothing.

She fought off the emotions with everything in her, and she joined the prince on the way downstairs.

The prince reached the main floor first and turned back toward her. "We'll find Hannah. It's all going to be okay."

Between the smoke and the dread, Cinderella didn't have a chance to respond before a gray, clawed hand appeared out of the darkness and slammed into the side of the prince's torso. Braedon flew halfway across the room and landed hard on his shoulder. As he grimaced in pain, the demon before them came into full view. Its gray skin was like armor. Its claws were even longer and sharper than the thief had realized. It stood tall and ugly and angry. Cinderella pulled out her sword. "What did you do to him?"

She let out a war cry that seemed to take the demon by surprise. Her sword moved as fast as lightning, but the beast's hands were quick, and its strong claws deflected the blade. Cinderella fought hard enough to back the creature away before she attempted to kick it in its midsection. Her foot met a surface as hard as stone. It didn't even move the demon a single inch.

The creature grinned and swiped for the thief's face. Cinderella barely feinted the blow, slicing her weapon along the beast's arm. Blood spurted onto the ground, and the creature shrieked. It backed away as the prince joined Cinderella. The blood looked and smelled human.

Cinderella wiped the crimson from her blade using her cloak as she prayed the massive gray creature wouldn't strike again. With a running charge, the demon dashed her hopes in a second. Before it could swing its claws toward the thief again, Braedon stepped up with his blade and met its claws.

He gritted his teeth and pushed hard with his back legs. "Go find the girl. I'm going to hold it off."

She shook her head. "No! I'm not going to leave you here with this."

The creature snarled, but the prince's strength repelled it backward. The beast shook its bleeding arm and cradled the injury.

Braedon shouted in the thief's direction. "I can handle this! Find the girl before it's too late."

Cinderella let out a guttural noise. "Fine. Be careful."

He let out a smile for a second. "Aren't I always?"

Cinderella held back a response and ran for the back room. On the way there, she could see smoke billowing up from under the door. She used her cloak on the door handle and could feel the heat straight through to her fingers. She took one last look back at Braedon and yanked the door open.

The room leading to Tristan's work area had flames crawling up the wall. She shoved down the painful memories of her past and crouched low as she moved toward the workroom.

Come on, Hannah. Please be alive.

Even with the cloak to protect her hands, the handle to the outside was burning hot. She yanked it open, but the cool outdoor breeze did little to defend Tristan's smithy, which was covered in red fiery streaks. She ignored every instinct that told her to run the opposite way and slammed her shoulder through the flame-covered front door.

Everything around her was shades of red, orange, and yellow. The heat was like nothing Cinderella had ever felt. She sweated from every pore and her vision blurred.

Her throat began to close up. "Hannah? Hannah!"

A faint voice called out from the other side of the room. "Elle!"

Cinderella pushed over a flaming worktable and sprinted until she saw the little girl hiding in the last untouched corner.

The moment of relief was fleeting. Without warning, one of the beams holding the building together toppled in front of their only exit.

There's no way out.

Hannah dashed from her hiding place over to Cinderella's side and gripped her leg hard. The thief tried to move to comfort her, but none of her muscles seemed to respond to their commands. Her chest tightened as she sunk to her knees. The flames continued to creep closer, threatening to burn the two of them alive.

PART 3

CHAPTER 21

The prince summoned up every tactic and memory he had of his years practicing with the sword. Fighting with Cinderella was one thing, but he knew he needed to be flawless to defeat some giant demon from most people's worst nightmare.

He tightened his grip around the hilt. "What's this all about, demon? Got tired of playing around in the sewers with the other grotesque trash of the town?"

If the creature understood that Braedon was trying to insult it, it didn't let on. The beast let go of its bleeding arm and crouched down into a defensive stance. Its breaths were loud, heavy, and terrifying.

The prince's heart had never beat this fast. "I'm not looking forward to killing you. Your head would make a terrible trophy on my wall."

He wasn't sure if the beast understood, but it let out a primal scream that shook every inch of the house.

The prince was glad he used the toilet earlier. His voice was less convincing this time. "Fine, no trophy. Cremation, then." As the creature lunged forward, the prince made his move to strike. His first swing was easily pushed aside by the beast's claws. Two more thrusts were likewise parried by the gray, hulking demon before him. He kicked off its midsection and retreated backward for another attack.

"Not planning to go down easy, I see."

He looked back at the direction Cinderella had gone. He listened for her voice or the sounds of the little girl. There was nothing but the crackling of the wood that would soon collapse around them.

"There'd better be a fifth date."

He turned his attention back to the demon and ran toward it again.

This time, the demon grabbed at his sword hand and pulled him in close. The foul breath of the creature shot out against his face as he struggled to avoid its teeth. The razor-sharp fangs were far too close for comfort.

As the prince struggled to get his hand free, he looked into the creature's eyes. Its very human eyes.

He stammered. "Your– you– look familiar."

Braedon stopped struggling for one moment too long, and the creature sank its teeth into his shoulder. The pain was deep and immediate, and he felt the top layer of flesh tear away from his body. He screamed in agony and used his feet to press away from the beast. He broke free when he relinquished his sword to the creature.

Braedon staggered back as far as possible and clutched at his wound. While he was bloody and suffering, the creature's teeth hadn't gone too deep into his shoulder itself.

"It could have ripped my arm off. He or she could have ripped my arm off."

The beast tossed the sword to the opposite end of the room and licked its bloody claws. It looked hungry for more.

The prince racked his brain to think of anything that would get him out of the situation. Before a single thought could form, the beast charged at him, and only a quick forward tumble got him out of the creature's grasp. He dashed across the room and stood by his sword. That's when a memory began to form.

The Godmother's voice played in his head. "As fast as you think you are, you can be 10 times faster. Just keep pushing past your limits."

The prince nodded and left his sword on the ground. "I can be faster. I can definitely be faster than this thing."

The creature charged again, but this time the prince was ready. He easily dodged a swipe of its claws and gave two swift kicks to its front leg. As it swung its clawed hand again, Braedon rolled underneath and got in three more kicks in rapid succession. The beast screamed and reached for the prince with both sets of claws. This threw it off balance, leaving a wide-open opportunity for Braedon to strike.

With all his might, the prince's foot connected with the creature's knee. Braedon began to smile as the creature staggered on a wobbly leg and favored the injuries the prince had dealt it.

"That crazy old woman was right. I can be faster!"

He crouched down and let loose a barrage of kicks and punches that were so swift, he wondered if the beast even saw them coming. Within moments, the creature went down to one knee, coming down to the prince's height. With an incredibly fast running shoulder, Braedon clocked the beast in the face. He could feel the impact of its skull all the way down his right arm, but this was no time for pain. It was time for victory.

The creature lost consciousness and fell chest-first onto the hardwood floor. Braedon pumped his fist in the air and screamed out his own war cry. Once again aware of his surroundings, the prince realized that the room had grown hotter. He looked toward the door Cinderella had used. Smoke was pouring in at double the previous rate.

"Damn."

When he looked back toward the beast he just defeated, the creature had completely disappeared. Nothing but the droplets of its very red blood remained as evidence of the battle that had just occurred. Braedon caught his breath and dashed outside toward the blacksmith's workspace. The heat was overwhelming, but a healthy dose of fear numbed him to the sensation. He reached the edge of the workroom, and his heart dropped. The entire front wall was covered in flames.

"Cinderella!"

There was no sound. There was no way in. There was nothing he could do.

CHAPTER 22

Cinderella could see her young arms and young hands before her face as clearly as if she were trapped in the past. Much like her current predicament, she was surrounded by unforgiving fire on every side. Her mother lay there before her, crumpled on the ground and breathless. She moved toward her lifeless mother and crouched beside the body she planned to join in death. With tears streaming down her face, a child's face, she took her mother's hand. Somehow amidst all the warmth that surrounded her, her mother's hand seemed almost frozen. She tightened her grip on the fingers and attempted to coax life back into them. It was no use. She tried to see her mother's face one more time before death, but hair covered her cheek and mouth and everything that would allow Cinderella to steal one more glance.

The squeeze of a small, childlike hand brought her back into the burning reality.

"Elle, are we going to die?"

Cinderella wasn't holding her mother's hand. She wasn't back in the building behind her stepmother's house that had burned to the ground so many years ago. She was in a new nightmare.

The thief looked deep into Hannah's eyes. "I don't know." She tightened her grip. "But I promise I won't leave you."

The blacksmith's daughter nodded and pressed her face into Cinderella's body.

The thief peered through the smoke and attempted to find another exit. Her heart continued to beat at a rapid pace, as if trying to get in as many thumps as possible before the inevitable struck. The heat could send them both to unconsciousness before the flames began to lick their bodies.

As she took a breath, she knew there was a good chance it could be one of the last ones.

The little girl gasped and pointed into the corner of the room. "Look!"

Cinderella's eyes shot open. Amid the floating embers and crumbling walls of the workroom, she spied a glimmering golden bird. She leaned toward the creature she'd seen the other day. Toward the creature who had been a part of her dreams.

But this was no dream. Her eyes darted as the bird zipped across the room and circled overtop an area she hadn't noticed before. Aside from where she and Tristan's daughter stood, it was the only space in the room that had yet to be touched by the flames. She couldn't believe she hadn't noticed it before.

Standing out among all the flames was a shining red light.

"The weapon!"

The thief pulled Tristan's daughter closer and crouched low as she stepped toward the beacon of hope. She sidestepped one fallen support beam, and then another. The little girl shrieked each time they got too close to the fire, but Cinderella knew she couldn't stop. She knew this was their only hope of survival.

The fire grew hotter the closer she got to the red jewel. It was embedded in the hilt of the last weapon the blacksmith had finished before the demon had taken the life from his eyes. Cinderella felt so much heat through her cloak, she wondered if it would catch fire and burn her body to a crisp.

"Not today. It's not happening again." Her words weren't convincing. Not even to herself. But she continued to move.

The thief reached the shining red weapon with a flying halo of gold over the top of it. Even though the flames completely surrounded them, Cinderella felt as if the temperature died down when she came within range of the weapon. Was it actually repelling the fire that threatened to end their lives? She set the girl down, seeing that her eyes were just as focused on the red jewel as the thief's were.

Cinderella took a deep breath and grabbed hold of Hannah's hand. With the other hand, she reached forward and took the sword.

A burst of air shot past the thief and flew in every direction. It was cool and refreshing and it sent energy through every part of Cinderella's body. The gust extinguished every flame it came into contact with, and within moments of her touching the weapon, all the fire in the room had been completely extinguished.

CHAPTER 23

The prince's eyes widened as the flames from the outside of the workroom evaporated in an instant. He stood there in silence for a few moments as he tried to understand the sight before him. He reached for the handle on the door with trepidation, but he soon realized it had returned to its normal temperature. He threw the door open and took everything in. The walls on either side were charred beyond recognition. Smokey beams from the roof piled up to his chest, giving him a small window into the scene that took place in the middle of the room. A girl he had to assume was the blacksmith's daughter had her head in Cinderella's lap. The thief brushed the girl's hair with the fingers of one hand while the other hand wrapped tightly around the hilt of a glowing, red weapon. The prince crouched down and slammed his healthy shoulder into a pile that blocked his entry. It took three tries, but he was able to knock down the impediment and walk into the room.

A weight lifted off his chest. "You're okay. I can't believe you're okay."

"You doubted me for even a second?" Even though the barb was expected, it didn't seem as though her heart was in it. She wasn't even looking at him; she was looking at something in the corner of the room.

Prince Braedon didn't care. He walked right up to her and stopped just short of giving the embrace his heart told him to initiate.

He rolled his bloody shoulder. "I knew you'd make it. I just thought I'd have another opportunity to save a girl in distress."

Her eyes moved to his. "You've come to the wrong place for damsels." She spied the blood on his neck. "The creature is gone?"

The prince nodded. "You should've seen me out there. The Godmother would've been proud."

She smiled and laid the now-sleeping Hannah onto the ground. She stood up and brushed a bit of ash from her shoulder. "I'm sure she would have given you a medal." She sighed. "Whatever that thing was, it sucked the life out of Tristan."

Braedon nodded in assent. "We need to get the whole army in here. They can scour the city and knock on every door, and–"

"Get their heads ripped off? You and I barely survived against that thing, and the soldiers who are left can't hold a candle to us. We need to trust a higher power."

The prince wrinkled his forehead. "Are you getting religious on me?"

Cinderella pointed back to the corner she'd been looking at when he first arrived. He was surprised he hadn't noticed it before. A glittering gold bird flapped its wings, as if to get attention. It was unlike anything Braedon had ever seen before.

"What is that?"

Cinderella stowed her weapon in her scabbard. "I'm not sure, but it's the only thing that saved me in here. I think I'm supposed to follow it."

The prince put his hands on his hips and turned away. "You're saying this bird is our only chance of stopping some ten-foot-tall demon?"

"Don't exaggerate. It was nine feet tall at most."

Braedon turned back. "Look, we figured out what was doing this. It's great that the magical bird or whatever helped you in here, but we need to get the army."

Cinderella pursed her lips and stepped right up to his chest. He could smell the smoke on her clothes.

"If you bring the army in here, it's going to be a bloodbath."

"If you follow some magical bird around, this creature is going to kill a dozen more people by the end of the night."

Cinderella grunted and poked Braedon with her finger. "We're not dealing with some common murderer. It's magical, so we need to focus on a magical way of defeating it. This sword may be the key."

The prince spun away and threw his hands up in the air. "Superpowered swords and birds that glitter with gold. You sound like a crazy person right now."

Cinderella's eyes narrowed.

Braedon could feel his temperature rising. Didn't she understand he just wanted her to be safe?

She picked up the blacksmith's daughter and put her over her shoulder. "I don't expect you to have faith in much of anything, Your Royal Highness. Unless it's at the bottom of a mug of ale."

The thief attempted to walk past him, but Braedon stuck out his arm to block her. "We've tracked this thing. Now we need help."

Cinderella glared at him with more fire than he'd seen on the walls of the workroom. "You're not involved in this anymore. Go to the tavern and drink yourself to death, for all I care. I need to explain to this girl that she's basically an orphan now, and then I need to figure out what the heck is going on. Don't show your face around this village and don't bring in innocent soldiers to die." She brought her face right up to his. "Am I understood?"

The prince didn't know how to feel. Part of him wanted to challenge the thief to another rooftop duel. The other part couldn't take his eyes off her lips.

"You are understood."

"Good." She stepped toward the path the prince had made with his shoulder. She paused when she got to the door and turned back to him. "Enjoy the ball, my Liege."

Braedon fumed as Cinderella walked out the door.

He stood there in silence for at least several minutes, hoping she would come to her senses and return. But no such thing happened. His chest felt like it was about to explode with rage, and he kicked at one of the broken beams.

"Dammit!" He took out several more raging blows of anger on the charred wood. "That girl is going to get herself killed!"

It was just then that the prince noticed the golden bird in the corner was staring at him. He screamed at it and waved his arms. The bird continued to perch there. With its tiny, golden eyes it appeared to comprehend exactly what was going on. The prince refused to believe his own eyes.

"There's no such thing as magic."

The bird appeared to smile, nod its head twice, and extend its wings before it flew out after Cinderella.

CHAPTER 24

It had been hours since Prince Braedon sat beside Kiyara on the bench of the royal garden, but she could still feel his warm touch even at the dark breeze of the village docks that surrounded her. She crouched beside a barrel of whiskey that she hoped was meant for some far-off land. Some place where her mother no longer had influence over her. Some place where she could be normal and not… some kind of abomination.

She'd shut out the memories of countless nights over the years for so long. But now, for some reason all the deeds she'd been compelled to perform while in a body of immense power were well within her grasp. The guilt was unbearable.

Kiyara saw all the people that her mother, her sister, and herself had destroyed over the years. Previously, she'd been able to block out the eyes from their faces, but now they were all coming back to her. And they were all so afraid. Afraid to look upon the grotesqueness she became when her mother laid hands upon her. Through bleary eyes, she looked down at her seemingly human arms and saw the scaled monstrosities they could become when provoked.

Her breaths were heavy. "There's something wrong with me. There's something wrong with all of us."

She heard several boatmen on the docks nearby. She prayed they wouldn't look in her direction. Her only hope to get away was to sneak onto one of the boats meant for the farthest corners of the world. She didn't even care if they took her back to the kingdom that had banished her family. She just needed to get away from all the people she had hurt. People she had ruined.

She clutched the money she'd stolen from her mother. Kiyara knew that if she got caught while attempting to stow away, there might be a way to bribe the men to silence. If they didn't assault her and toss her in the water first.

The butterflies within her stomach had wings of razors, and they cut into the tender lining inside her. Each breath came with a painful tightness, and she wished she had the bravery of her true sister Cinderella beside her.

Kiyara sensed an opening onto the diagonal plank that would lead her to freedom. "Elle wouldn't hesitate. Elle would go forward and never look back."

She balled up her fists and made a break for it. Though her shoes were clunkier than she'd hoped, their soft bottoms failed to give away her position. None of the boatmen turned to see her run onto a ship cloaked with darkness. She took the only open door on the galley and looked for a place to hide, but her eyes had yet to adjust to the dark. She bumped into several walls before finding a door that gave way from the push of her shoulder. She closed the entrance behind her and leaned back against it until her eyes got used to the level of light. Slowly but surely, she could see she'd wandered into a storage area where multiple barrels were bound for places unknown.

"This could work. They might not find me for hours."

She used her hands to feel at the thick wooden casks around her. She traced them all the way to the far end of the room, where a large stack of the cargo could easily conceal her. She moved behind them, placing the highest barrel between her and the entrance before she sat down and waited.

Kiyara tried to piece the last decade of her life together in her mind. She had once lived in the castle. Yes, she and her older sister Malina were princesses of a sort. The images of her childhood were spotty at best, but they were completely carefree until her mother had been overthrown.

Her heart mimicked the pace it had taken when she and her sister were ushered out of the only home she'd ever known in the middle of the night. She hadn't been able to take any of her toys or other possessions. All she had left was a sister who ignored her and a mother who always had better things to do.

So much of their journey away from her home was a blur all these years later. She remembered her mother waking in the middle of the night and screaming. Malina was the first to offer to take her pain, but the pain changed her when it spread through her body. And when it was too much for one sister to handle, Kiyara was volunteered.

The door opened and Kiyara's heart skipped a beat. She held her breath and listened. Two grown men bantered back and forth as they carried several more barrels into the room.

"How many ships you think they could get for what they're spending on that fancy ball?"

The other man laughed. "The queen could buy this ship, me, you, and half the fleet before she was done. And that would just pay for the food."

They laughed together and slammed several more casks into the place. Kiyara let out a small breath and regretted the noise she made.

"You know, we could always push the shipment one night. Try to get a last second ticket and dance with any maidens Prince Braedon rejects. What do you think?"

Kiyara gripped the nearest barrel with her fingers.

The other man scoffed. "We have about as much of a chance of getting into that ball as this ship has flying to the moon. And looking at that face of yours makes me think that the moon has a much higher chance."

The two of them roared with laughter and slammed the door behind them.

Kiyara let herself breathe normally again. "It's leaving tonight. This ship is leaving tonight and you're going to be okay."

The time seemed to creep by incredibly slowly. She noticed the gentle shifting of the boat beneath her and timed her breath to it. Everything in her world stood still until the boat lurched to life. She wasn't sure how long she held her breath, but when she finally took in air again, she knew the ship was moving.

Tears welled in her eyes as she hoped it would continue for years until she'd gotten away from a life she hated. From a life she'd never chosen in the first place. It was at the peak of her hope that the boat came to a complete stop. Over the sounds of the water that leapt across the sides of the ship, she heard a scream. And then another. Her heart leapt at each one. After their voices died down, silence painted everything.

Kiyara tucked her head between her knees and started to rock. She only stopped when the door to the storage room opened. Malina's sickly sweet scent was apparent immediately. She could almost hear the smile upon her sister's face.

"I know you're in there, Kiyara. I can smell you, too." Her laugh echoed ominously throughout the room. "She's in here, Mother."

Heavy footsteps wandered into the room and a light glow illuminated everything. Kiyara knew her efforts had been for nothing. She stood up and watched her family come into view.

Armenia shook her head. "Since when did my obedient little flower become so insolent?"

"I'm sorry, Mother."

"Do you know how much power I had to expend to find you? If I hadn't dined on the blacksmith's heart today, I might've run out. You know that I'm saving up everything for the ball."

Kiyara nodded. "I know."

Armenia's hand glowed a bright red. Her lips curled into a smile. "The biggest surprise is that the prince actually seems to like you."

Malina crossed her arms, revealing a bandage caked with blood upon one of her forearms.

Kiyara stuttered. "I– I don't think he likes me. Of course, he likes Malina much better."

Armenia put her hand around Kiyara's lower back.

"Don't be modest, my dear, sweet flower." Her hand began to grow hot on Kiyara's skin. "Your approach was a little more effective."

Malina scowled. "He'll change his tune. Just wait until he sees me in that dress."

Kiyara felt her mother's hand growing hotter.

Armenia pressed her hand deeper into the flesh. "Regardless of who he chooses, our plan won't work if you're in another kingdom."

Kiyara wanted to scream out in pain as the burn began to form on her lower back. "I'm sorry, Mother. I promise I won't do it again."

Armenia let her hand linger upon her daughter's back for a moment or two longer before withdrawing.

Kiyara almost collapsed but kept herself upright by grabbing one of the barrels. "Thank you. Thank you."

Her mother admired her handiwork, a perfectly tattooed handprint right on her daughter's back. "I believe you. Let's just not get into any more trouble, shall we?"

Kiyara nodded and grimaced as the air made her skin burn.

Malina wrinkled her nose. "Can we get out of here? It's starting to smell like rotten fish and dead bodies."

Armenia grabbed Kiyara's shoulder so abruptly that the girl forgot how to breathe.

Armenia's red eyes stared straight into hers. "You will obey me, Daughter. Or I will burn your stepsister Cinderella to death in her sleep."

Kiyara got the message loud and clear.

CHAPTER 25

The thief and the blacksmith's daughter walked quietly through the night. The blood in Cinderella's veins continued to pulse quickly, though more from the conversation with the prince than from her fight with the grotesque demon. She wished the prince were right in front of her and that she could punch him in the face for wanting to bring innocents into this magical battle. But she knew that Hannah had seen enough tonight. The thief shook off her annoyance and focused her attention back on the blacksmith's daughter.

"It's going to be okay."

Hannah sniffled. "It doesn't sound like you believe that."

Cinderella huffed and remembered a day when she could convince Tristan's daughter of anything. "You're right. I'm not convinced. But I'm not so sure that what I believe matters anymore."

Hannah looked up at her with wide, brown, watery eyes. "What do you mean?"

Cinderella turned them down a dim alley. "I thought for a long time that my father had forgotten how to love me. That he chose not to love me anymore. Now with these demons and fires and magical swords, I'm not sure if I was right." The thief reached her destination and knelt down on one knee. "But I can be sure that the Godmother and I are going to take very good care of you until we figure out what's going on."

Hannah took in a deep breath. "Does that mean my dad is going to love me again?"

The thief looked up and wondered how often her late mother had to answer tough questions like this when Cinderella was a child. "For a long time, I would've said no. But now, I'm changing my answer to 'I hope so.'"

The Godmother appeared at the entryway to her house and Hannah ran into her outstretched arms. The little girl had been on the verge of tears since they left Tristan's home. It was as if she didn't want the thief to see her crying. Now she let it all loose.

Cinderella stayed on the ground and looked into her mentor's eyes. There was sympathy there, but also a sense of determination. The Godmother didn't seem like she'd be satisfied by picking up the pieces. Like Cinderella, she probably wanted revenge, too.

"I heard about what happened."

Cinderella shook her head. "Of course you did." She touched the hilt of the red-jeweled sword. "How did you know this would protect me?"

The Godmother almost smiled. "It's one part of a puzzle that only you can put together. I think you already know where to find the next piece." She looked up and Cinderella followed her gaze.

Circling in the air and looking quite impatient was the golden bird from her past, her present, and perhaps the future salvation of the kingdom.

Cinderella stood. "Are you truly as in the dark as I am, or do you know how this all ends and you're just toying with me?"

The Godmother stroked the back of Hannah's head. "Some answers work best when you find them out on your own. I'm going to take her to bed."

Cinderella smirked. "And I guess I'm going bird-watching."

The thief was thankful for the bird's quick pace, which forced her to run at almost top speed, keeping most of her thoughts at bay. Every time it seemed that the prince or Kiyara came into her mind, the golden bird made a sudden jerk left or right, and Cinderella was forced to drop all of her worries to quickly change her direction. Her legs started to burn from the strain, and she loved how strong the sheer amount of effort she put in made her feel.

The bird took Cinderella out of the village proper and past a small network of canopied forests. Small woodland creatures scampered away as she went by.

Soon enough, the bird rested above the mouth of a large, deep cave. The golden creature mercifully let Cinderella catch her breath and stretch out her legs after testing her endurance. The rapid beating of her heart and full exertion of her limbs only allowed for trickles of Tristan the blacksmith, Prince Braedon, and Kiyara to enter her mind. As she examined the lip of the cave, she realized the Godmother used to take her here for training runs in the dark. It was one of the ways she developed her near-perfect vision under the moonlight. After all, she learned to fight in the pitch black of the musty and slippery cave. While many travelers might require a lantern or other source of light to enter into the darkness, even a little light was more than enough for her.

But this time, Cinderella didn't just have night vision. She had a glowing golden bird to light the way.

The creature seemed to smile as it flew headlong into the gaping hole. Cinderella descended into the cavern and wondered how she'd suppressed this golden icon from her memory for so long. She'd never seen such a thing before her mother's death, and she hadn't seen it again until the last few nights. Either it was coincidence or something big was about to happen.

Cinderella had lost all track of time when the bird fluttered its wings and rested before a fork between two caves.

"You know which way you're going?"

The bird nodded so quickly and assertively that Cinderella knew it understood her words.

She shook her head. "Thank you for saving my life. Twice, I guess."

She'd never seen a bird smile until now.

"What am I going to find in here?"

The bird paused for a moment, as if trying to determine how to convey the upcoming danger. Then it made a motion with its wing as if pulling something out from its hip. When Cinderella mirrored the motion, she came right into contact with the hilt of the jeweled sword. When the bird nodded, Cinderella knew it was time to draw her weapon.

"I'm not sure how you understand me, or how you're doing what you're doing. But I hope you're not getting me killed tonight."

The bird was a little more solemn than the thief expected. Was the golden creature worried the thief wasn't up for the task? It portrayed no further trepidation as it left off its perch and chose the path to the right. Cinderella had no choice but to follow.

After what must've been an hour of silence in the cave, Cinderella was surprised to hear voices echoing through the cavern. The golden bird flew just high enough that it was able to illuminate all the way to one of the guards who stood watch.

But what is he watching?

The thief looked to the bird, who'd found a jagged rock to perch upon as it closed its wings and dulled its colors. Now the only light came from what seemed like a far-off lantern beyond the unsuspecting guard. But he wasn't the one talking.

Cinderella hid behind one of the folds of the cave and listened.

"I can't believe she has us stuck in here, so far away from the action. It's almost like she's punishing us or something."

A higher-pitched voice laughed. "I'm not surprised. I'd take one look at you and punish you as much as I could."

The thief heard the two men pushing each other as the first guard, who seemed to want nothing to do with the rabble, stayed completely silent.

Cinderella once again glanced up to the bird, whose body was pointed straight past the guards. The creature nodded intelligently for emphasis.

She sighed internally. "I guess this is the part where I trust the magical bird to lead me somewhere important." She withdrew her red-jeweled sword. "I've had worse informants."

She looked up and returned the nod to the animal. Without a moment's hesitation, the bird let its wings fly loose and bask the entire cave in gold.

The guard in front who had an accent Cinderella didn't recognize turned back and shouted. "We need a net. The other twin is back."

When the foreigner turned around, Cinderella was right there to meet him. "Good evening."

The guard's eyes went wide as he tried to draw his sword from his scabbard, but the thief was much too quick for that. With one slice she ripped the sword from his hip and it clattered to the ground. With a sideways swing she clocked the guard in the side of his helmet. The sheer force of the blow sent him to the ground unconscious. The other two guards came running toward her. One of them had a net in his hand.

The high-pitched guard with a long wooden staff stopped and spoke first. "Who the heck are you?"

She tightened her grip on the hilt. "Loren Bird Preservation Society. I have a feeling you two are violating a few of our codes."

His grunt sounded like a teenage girl getting flustered, and he charged at her with his weapon.

She shook her head and timed her sword just right. The expert blade cut through his staff like butter. When it broke in two, the guard was so off-balance that the thief merely needed to stick out her foot for the man to trip over. He ended up with a face full of dust on the ground of the cave. Cinderella turned toward the guard with the net. She watched as he eyed the golden bird acting like an upper-class lantern in the corner.

The thief changed her grip and pulled the sword over her shoulder. "I don't think so."

With a mighty throw, Cinderella's sword zipped across the room and penetrated the guard's net. The throw was so strong that it wrenched the device from his hands and pinned the net to the wall, where it stuck in at least a foot deep.

The empty-handed guard cried out. "What are you doing?"

Cinderella shrugged. "Winning?"

The man rushed for her and she easily feinted both off-kilter punches. With lightning-quick speed, she took the man's head with both of her hands and brought it down to her knee. She felt his nose crunch from the impact.

The man yelped in pain and tried to stop the bleeding with his palm. Cinderella whipped her body around and kicked him in the side of the helmet. With a satisfying clank, the guard fell to the ground.

As Cinderella pulled her sword from the stone of the cave's wall, she heard a sound she was hoping to avoid. The golden bird flew down from its perch and landed on the thief's shoulder.

"That noise better not be what I think it is."

The bird seemed to form an apologetic gesture with its face. Cinderella crouched down in a stance of readiness, shifting her feet back and forth.

"What they're guarding better be worth it."

The sound of at least a dozen more guards approached, and the thief felt a smile taking over her face.

CHAPTER 26

Prince Braedon looked down at the bottom of another drink. Like the three he'd had before it, it was as empty as he felt. At least it numbed the pain from his shoddily patched shoulder wound. He placed the mug down on the counter, and the only thing that brought him out of his head was a mighty slap on the back from Falstone.

The gargantuan knight bellowed with laughter. "The only way through heartbreak, my boy, is to have about six more of those." He gestured to the man behind the counter. "Three more of what he's having. Two for me and one for him."

The prince's head began to spin. It appeared that even two days without booze had made him a little more susceptible. "I don't think I should have any more."

Falstone's eyes grew large. "Blasphemy. Utter blasphemy, Your Royal Highness. My dearest friend, let me ask you something. Are you still sad?"

Braedon thought back to the burning building and the deep, painful feeling that he wouldn't see Cinderella again. He'd never felt that way about any of the highborn ladies who had strutted their way around the castle. He'd never felt that way about any of the beautiful servants and other employees of the queen. And now he was drinking his way into oblivion because of a common thief.

The prince wanted to lie, but his face already betrayed his feelings. "Yes, Falstone. I am sad, and I appreciate you continuing to remind me."

"If you're sad, then you should obviously keep drinking. It's the only way to stop it."

The prince wasn't sure which gave him more of a headache, Falstone's loud voice or the drinks that were working their way through his brain and body. "I'm not sure if that's the prescription for me today."

Falstone let his meaty paw rest upon the prince's uninjured shoulder. "I'm not here to pressure you, my boy. If you don't want to drink, we can go paint the town red in plenty of other ways. Why, I know this brothel–"

Braedon shrugged Falstone's hand away. "Maybe I don't want to get my mind off her just yet."

Falstone chuckled softly. Then the laugh grew and grew in volume until the man's face was as red as Braedon had ever seen it. "He's in love. The prince is in love!" Falstone stood up and raised one of his new drinks into the air. "Everybody, my best friend is head over heels in love!"

The dozen or so patrons throughout the room, who were in various stages of intoxication, stood with their drinks in the same position and cheered.

The prince buried his face in his hands. "I am not in love, Falstone. I don't even know if this girl likes me back."

Falstone wrapped his arm around Braedon and pulled him in tight as if he were telling the prince a secret. "You are quite the catch, my boy. Why, if my thoughts weren't overcome by the beautiful bodies of women from sunrise to... well, the next sunrise, then I would even say you are handsome."

Braedon rolled his eyes. "Thanks, I guess."

"Plus, the fact that you're rich and powerful works in your favor. If this Cindy person doesn't see you in that way, then she's probably crazy."

Braedon looked away. "She's different. She might be crazy." He shook his head. "And I yelled at her."

Falstone nodded. "We've all been there. When in the company of a fine lady, I've probably said more wrong things than right. Maybe only wrong things, and that's why I'm here with you." He laughed uproariously once again and downed half of his drink in a single swig.

The prince tried to take in enough oxygen to shake the fog from his brain. "Maybe it's not even worth thinking about all of this. After all, there are demons running around town taking my mother's men out of the picture. What's the point of thinking about the future when some creature might slice your throat the next day?"

Falstone pulled at his beard and began to stroke it. "You have it all wrong, my boy. When it looks like the end is near, that is when you absolutely need to take action."

The prince leaned toward him.

Maybe the sloppy drunk is right.

He pushed his drink away. "Okay. Okay, I'll say something to her."

Falstone finished the rest of his drink. "There's a good egg. And after all, choosing a woman is like choosing just one type of ale. At some point you're going to get bored, so you may as well drink as much of that first drink as you can, until the inevitable moment comes." He took another drink in his hands. "When the next drink is available."

Braedon rubbed at his left temple. "Great advice as always, Falstone."

The old drunk smiled a toothy grin. "I really should charge for it, shouldn't I?" He stared off across the room. "I've changed more people's lives than I can think of."

The prince pushed his drink in front of Falstone. "Indeed you have, my friend. Indeed you have."

The sound of a throat clearing caused the prince to turn around. The Queen's messenger looked as out of place as Falstone would at a fancy tea party.

"I have an important message for you, Your Highness."

Before the prince could say a word, Falstone moved with more agility than Braedon thought possible and snatched the note from the messenger's hand.

Falstone tore off the royal seal. "My good man, I'll be reading this correspondence to the future king. But first, can you tell me if it is good news or bad news? I like to make sure I'm in character."

The messenger shrunk in discomfort. "I'm afraid it's bad news. Very bad."

The prince felt his pulse quicken. "Has there been another attack?" He chewed his cheek. "I knew I shouldn't have come here. I should have been out in the city protecting people–"

"It's your mother." Falstone fumbled with the paper and handed it to Braedon. "Maybe you should read it after all."

The prince's eyes scanned the message and his shoulders slumped even more. He looked at the messenger. "Where is she?"

"In her chambers. I can take you to her right now."

The prince stepped off his chair and stood up straight. "Okay."

As the two of them made to leave, Falstone called after them. "Braedon!"

Braedon turned back.

"Are you sure you don't want one for the road?"

The prince sighed. "My mother is dying, Falstone. I think I should be sober for this."

CHAPTER 27

Cinderella let a calm settle over her body and mind as she considered the approaching guards in the cave. She thought back to all the lessons the Godmother had taught her over the last decade. She'd use the wise words of her mentor to take down groups of three, like the men who lingered on the ground, and angry mobs of up to seven in her time. But a dozen was a new story. A dozen in a dimly lit cave might be even more of a challenge.

She let the Godmother's voice play in her head as the world slowed down around her. "It's the vanity of men that makes them weak. They always feel the need to show themselves as stronger than their compatriots. When a fight presents incredible odds, exploiting this weakness is your only path to victory."

Cinderella internalized the wisdom and let her cloak fall to the ground, leaving just her light leather tunic and pants. Her long blonde hair untucked itself and fell down upon her shoulders. The charging group of men stopped in their tracks. The lead guard, who sported one of the most disgusting smiles the thief had ever seen, put his teeth on display.

His yellowed grin contrasted against the glow of the bird. "Hello, pretty thing. Wander in from the whorehouse, did you?"

Cinderella stepped into the middle of the cavern, the area with the most space possible.

Please, please, fight me one at a time.

She raised the pitch of her voice to sound more feminine. "Maybe I did. But it looks like you're not enough of a man to take me on by yourself."

The unpolished smile turned into a growl. He put one arm up and gestured for the other men to back away. "This one thinks she's funny. I think I'm gonna be the one to teach her a lesson."

She crouched down and readied herself, keeping the smile that wanted to form upon her face internal. "I'm ready when you are."

The man with the ugly smile came running, his sword held high. As he came to thrust it down at her, she easily sidestepped his lumbering swing. She kicked him hard in the midsection, and his unpadded tunic wasn't nearly strong enough to withstand the blow. She let her leg fly unencumbered straight into his crotch. The man crumpled to the ground in pain as the thief finished the contest with a leaping punch in the back of his head.

She stood up and tried to look more winded than she actually was. "Who's next?"

Another solo competitor, this one with two daggers instead of a sword, circled around her. He was quicker than his disgusting companion, but he relied too much on his weapons. Two expertly placed kicks to his wrists sent the knives scraping across the ground. When he tried to recover them, Cinderella used his momentum to carry him head-first into the unforgiving wall of the cave.

She heard a squawk from behind her as one of the other guards nearly got a hold of the golden bird. The thief took one of the daggers and intentionally whizzed it by the man's head. As he turned to avoid it, he left himself wide open for a blazingly fast kick to the side. The cracking sound made Cinderella know that she'd broken at least one rib. As she stepped back to the middle of the room, she was down to nine guards remaining, but it appeared as though they had learned their lesson.

Three guards approached, attempting to flank her on either side.

Cinderella thought back to the day the Godmother had given her the lesson on male vanity.

As precocious as she always was, Cinderella had asked more than a few questions.

"And what if they start teaming up anyway?"

The Godmother's neutral face was burned into her memory. "Then you divide and conquer."

The thief faked toward one of the men and sprinted at full speed toward one of the others. She caught him completely off-guard and ducked under a halfhearted swipe of his sword. She tucked her arm under his and tossed him across the room and into his two partners. Under the weight of their friend, they stumbled backward and slammed hard into the remaining men who were there to fight her. She took the momentary respite to gesture at the bird to run in the direction the guards had come from. Somehow, the golden creature took the hint and Cinderella followed.

The thief smiled as she ran. "Time to thin out the herd."

As soon as she felt one of the guards approaching, Cinderella darted right and ran with incredible speed up the side of one of the caves. She just avoided his grasp and performed a sideways flip in the air before scissor-kicking him in the neck. The moment she landed, she continued running. When another guard got close, she split-kicked backward right between the man's eyes without stopping her stride. He grunted as his body slammed to the ground.

Four to go.

Cinderella felt strong. She knew that after all this running and fighting, it should have taken some kind of toll on her body. Instead, she felt ready for anything. As two additional guards approached her from the rear, she lifted her sword sideways and with one fluid motion spun and cracked both of them across the face with it. The two of them were out on their feet as Cinderella took their helmets and bashed them into one another, sending them reeling to the ground.

The thief felt electric as she saw a familiar glimmering light in the direction she was heading. She noticed the bird fly faster, and she did everything she could to catch up. When she finally reached the end of the tunnel, Cinderella's jaw dropped. There, in a cage of bone, was an exact replica of the bird who had led her here. It glimmered in the same gold as the bird that now circled its cage overhead. The two creatures began to chirp at one another.

Cinderella pursed her lips. "If this was all just to get you and your best friend back together, I might be pissed."

Her observation of the friendly bird moment allowed one of the two remaining guards to swing at her. She ducked the blow by less than an inch and then turned to face one of the largest men she'd ever seen. At least, until his slightly bigger compatriot reached his side.

They were out of breath, but she had a feeling their lungs weren't the reason they'd been recruited. Cinderella snapped her leg toward one of the hulking giants and kicked him in the midsection. The man didn't even stumble. She was so surprised at his lack of backward motion that she wasn't prepared for him to swing his fist and strike her in the side of the jaw. Pain cracked through her face as her head whipped back. She rubbed at the forming bruise as the two guards approached.

One of them spoke with a deep, rumbling voice. "You won't be taking her prize. And you won't be leaving here alive."

The thief tasted blood as she let her tongue play against her teeth. "You may not know this about me, but I'm not so good at following the rules."

She waited until the two guards were in perfect position next to one another before she pretended to swing her sword toward their faces. As they reached for the large hammers they concealed behind their backs, Cinderella made her real move. She sliced her blade downward, targeting the ankles of the ridiculously large guards. She truly appreciated how close the two were standing together when the sword met its targets of one guard's right ankle and the other guard's left. The weapon cut deep enough on both to penetrate armor and skin. The guards' deep screams rumbled through the cave.

One of them dropped his weapon and leaned forward. Cinderella threw three quick body blows followed by an uppercut so powerful, she surprised even herself. The punch hit the beast of a man right under the chin and sent him to the ground. The remaining bleeder swung off-balance with his hammer, which sent him spinning away from her as the weapon hit the ground.

The thief took the opportunity to leap upon his back and lock her hands around his neck in what the Godmother had always called an unbreakable chokehold. The guard swung his body wildly, which only put more pressure on his sliced ankle. He stumbled to the ground chest-first and landed with a stone-cracking fall.

Cinderella tightened her grip as the man attempted to reach backwards, but his muscles were far too big, giving him the flexibility of a rock.

She could feel the man starting to slow down in her grasp. "The bigger they are, the harder and dumber they fall."

The guard's limbs slackened until the man was completely unconscious. She relinquished his grasp and wiped the sweat from his neck off on her tunic. She grinned. "If only the old mare could've seen me in action."

She heard the squawking of two very real birds back at the cage. She stepped toward them. Cinderella was amazed that such a magical creature, which she assumed was completely unique, had its own duplicate right before her.

"You better back up, bird #2. I'm gonna get you out of there. And hope this all wasn't just a waste of my time."

The new bird seemed to have the same level of comprehension as the first, and it politely moved backward away from the side of the cage. With a well-placed blow, Cinderella smashed through the bone cage and provided an opening just large enough for the bird to fly out of. She expected the birds to fly around and chirp like crazy. Instead, they calmly perched atop the cage and embraced each other as if they were hugging.

She rubbed at one of her eyes. "Maybe Braedon is right. Maybe I have gone crazy. Bird crazy. The worst kind."

When the two flying friends had finished their reunion, one of them chirped to get the thief's attention. As it did, it held up one of its feet, and Cinderella noticed for the first time there was some kind of binding around its leg. The other bird displayed its appendage as well, which had the exact same shackle upon it.

Without hearing a single word, Cinderella knew exactly what she had to do. She took out her sword and slowly but surely snipped the bindings on each of the birds. In unison, they let out a gleeful squawk as they fluttered to the ground together. With a noise that was almost musical, the birds began to transform. Cinderella stepped backward as she watched the two shimmering creatures turn into young girls with golden hair and dresses.

Cinderella's mouth gaped open. "By the gods."

One of the girls put her hands together and smiled. "You asked if she was my best friend. Actually, she's my sister."

CHAPTER 28

Prince Braedon hopped every second step in the castle on the way up to his mother's bedroom. As he ran, his heart clattering around in his chest, he couldn't help but let a thousand thoughts go through his head at once.

She can't be dying. I won't allow it. If she dies....

Braedon tried to shake the fear from his mind. He'd just seen her and she was perfectly fine. If the demon had something to do with this, he would paint the village with blood to find and destroy it.

He continued leaping over steps until he reached the main corridor.

If I become king, there'll be no more bars. No more friendships. Maybe even no more Cinderella.

He fought against the pain that last thought brought him as he sprinted down the hallway and toward his mother's room.

I can't bear to see her dying. After Father, I just–

He yanked the door open with a grunt. He bounded across the room to his mother's bedside. But she wasn't there. The bed looked as if it had been freshly made. His breath left him for a moment as he feared the worst.

"Was I too late?"

The prince looked left and right and tried to collect himself. Braedon ran into the hall and started calling out for a servant. For anybody. Eventually, he heard voices coming from his own room. In his frenzy, he couldn't recognize them. Did they belong to a doctor and a coroner? Were they starting to make funeral arrangements?

The prince felt mad as he ran back down the hallway and into his chambers.

As he attempted to catch his breath in the doorway, the first thing he noticed in the room was his mother. Not only was she standing, but she also appeared to be in perfect health.

Her cheeks glowed with pink. "Ah, there you are my son. So nice of you to be on time for your fitting."

Sure enough, the queen wasn't alone. Standing next to her was a tailor getting ready to take his measurements.

Fear changed to rage within. "I thought you were dying. I thought you were dead."

The queen nodded slightly. "And I'm touched that you didn't stay for three or four more drinks before you returned home, but I'm afraid there was no other way to get you to rush home with the speed you needed unless I lied to you."

The prince punched the wall with such ferocity that he made it all the way through the plaster.

He gripped his hair with both hands. "I can't believe you did that to me." He tried to burn fire through his eyes toward his mother, but she met him with a smile.

He shook his head. "That's it. I'm not going to the ball. It's official."

As he turned to walk away, he noticed five royal guards standing between him and the exit.

He felt a hand upon his shoulder.

The queen's fingers massaged at the muscle. "I'm sorry, Braedon. But if my impending death was the only way to get you in, then my army has to be the only thing to keep you here."

Braedon wished he could be anywhere but here. The place he most wanted to be, for the first time in a long while, wasn't the bar. He wished he could be trying to land just one more blow on the unsuspecting Cinderella.

He put up his hands. "Fine, I'll stay. But whatever it is that's attacking your soldiers, it isn't human."

He pulled back his sleeve to reveal bloodstained cloth that protected his wound. "Something is out there, Mother." He gestured to the claw marks. "And I barely escaped it with my life."

She looked up at him, as if trying to determine his level of trustworthiness. "And how do I know you didn't get these marks fighting against a rabid animal while drunk?"

Braedon pounded at the wall again and began to pace the length of the room. "First, you get me here under false pretenses. Then you call me a liar. Why is that fair?"

The queen crossed her arms. "For the last year, this was the only night I actually needed you to be a part of. You begged and negotiated away so many of the moments we could've spent together, but this was the day you promised you would be here." If she felt any contrition for her lie, she certainly wasn't showing it. "This is not the time for stories, Braedon. It's the time to start living the responsibility of a boy who will be a king. It's time to become a man."

Braedon wanted to scream, but instead he sat down on the edge of his mattress. "I'll go to the ball."

The queen smirked. "What was that? I couldn't hear you, it was so quiet and meek."

"I'll go to the damn ball! But I'm not lying about the creature. I think we're all in great danger."

The queen nodded. "Then it's good that we've doubled the guards to keep you from escaping. They'll do the duty of looking out for any figments of your imagination as well."

The prince wanted to send a messenger to Cinderella right then. But he knew the words of a thief, especially one who stole a jewel from the queen's possession, would not do much to improve his chances of proving himself.

"Just make sure everybody is on watch. I'm not interested in letting somebody die just because you don't trust me."

His mother seemed taken aback by his tone. "I'll tell them. Now, why don't you let yourself get measured and get that cut taken care of so it doesn't bleed into your suit?"

The prince nodded. "Yes, Mother."

The queen stepped out of the room, and the five guards she placed to watch him took her place.

Braedon walked up to the tailor and held his arms out, feeling very much like he had no control whatsoever.

He looked out the window in the direction of the village. "Be careful out there, Elle."

CHAPTER 29

Cinderella marveled at the young identical girls standing in front of her. They sparkled with gold, as they did in their bird form. She had no earthly idea what to say.

One of the twins spoke. "Thank you for saving us. It's been so long since we've been able to return to this form."

Cinderella stammered. "So long– what do you– you aren't really little girls are you?"

The first girl held out her hand. "I'm Aymee, and this is my sister Tressa. Don't worry, we'll explain everything."

Cinderella took her hand, and Tressa took the other one. The twins stood on either side of her and started to lead the way out of the cave.

The thief and the two young girls walked through the cave between the groaning, injured men. She was surprised that none of them got back up after she'd fought them, but when she noticed a glowing gold above the heads of the fallen, she realized that magic was at work.

"I have a feeling I'm not going to understand much of what happens from here on out."

The girls squeezed her hands in unison and the one named Aymee spoke. "You know more than you realize. You followed the signs and you have the jewel. Now all you need is the truth."

Cinderella held her breath. Somehow she knew that these girls were about to fill the gap in her knowledge that the Godmother had intentionally left for so many years.

"You know the Godmother. She never spoke of you."

Tressa, who the thief could only distinguish by the fact that she was on her opposite side, made a little laugh. "We know more than we let on. It's surprising how much a prisoner can hear. Especially when a human watching over her doesn't think she's very smart."

Cinderella nodded. "Men are idiots sometimes. How about you start by telling me what the heck you are?"

The girls giggled again, which made Cinderella feel brighter as they walked through the dark cavern.

Aymee cleared her throat. "We're changers. We can switch our form whenever we want, unless someone takes measures to block it. We've been trapped in our bird form for quite some time.

"We also make dresses. Kinda like the ones we're wearing."

Cinderella sighed. "Everybody needs a hobby, I guess. Who captured you?"

"The former queen of our land. She was exiled, but she did a lot of damage on the way out. When we tried to find out where she was, she captured us."

Aymee picked up where her sister left off. "She was an awful, terrible woman who used magic to bend people to her will instead of helping them."

"If Aymee hadn't escaped, we would have no way to warn you of what's coming."

Cinderella sensed the moonlight as they got closer to the cave's entrance. "What can this queen do, exactly? Is she the one that's been building herself up like a demon? Is that her?"

The twins both took part in a pointed pause before Aymee spoke. "Cinderella, you might want to sit down for this."

"I'm fine standing. Just tell me everything."

The girls released Cinderella's hands and stood before her, silhouetted in the light from the stars and moon.

"Anyone who opposed the queen met a terrible fate."

"She would have their loved ones tortured in front of them."

"As soon as they felt pain in their heart, the queen could touch them and suck everything out."

"All the good. All the bad. And then soon as she was finished, it was like they had nothing left. Their hearts had been sucked dry."

The thief's pulse quickened. The realization of 10 years fell on her all at once. "My father was one of the first victims in this village, wasn't he?"

The twins nodded in unison.

Cinderella let out a slow-metered breath. "He never stopped loving me. He just had his heart pulled out of him."

The twins nodded in unison.

"And Armenia was the queen. You're telling me Armenia was the queen, right?"

The twins paused before affirming her question.

Cinderella wanted to tear the entire world apart. The anger took hold of every cell in her body. Her screams echoed through the chamber as she thrashed her arms every which way. She would have smashed her hands into the stone walls of the cave if she didn't know deep down that she would soon have to use them again.

Cinderella covered her face before letting her fingers stream through her blonde hair. "That's why Kiyara's charm was there. Armenia isn't the demon. She turns my stepsisters into… whatever they are. I am such an idiot."

Aymee stepped forward. "It's okay. You were just a girl, and you didn't realize that—"

"That the woman who destroyed my life was also the one who killed my mother. And who knows how many others."

Aymee's lip quivered. "We're sorry. But one of the reasons we saved you so many years ago was that we knew you had the strength to defeat her."

Cinderella let the rage settle and exit through her body. A few deep breaths had her almost back to normal. "Part of me has always wished I died in that fire. That I died with my mother's arms wrapped around me." She cracked her knuckles. "I guess life just isn't that simple. How about you tell me how I kill this horrible creature?"

Tressa rubbed her hands together. "On that front, we have some good news."

Aymee smiled. "When our kingdom needed to expel the queen, our mages devised a gem that can resist her power. We called it the Heartstone."

The thief pulled out her sword, which glistened red in the moonlight. "That's why the sword put out the fire. That's why the Godmother and Tristan both thought it was so important."

The twins agreed. "It's the only weapon against her. You're the best chance of stopping the queen from taking over another kingdom."

Cinderella held the jewel of the weapon to her forehead. She could feel the magical energy emanating from the stone.

She took one more deep breath and placed the weapon back in its scabbard. "Tonight, we plan. Tomorrow, it's time for revenge."

CHAPTER 30

A day had gone by since Kiyara had seen any trace of her stepsister. Her mother had raised a fuss for about fifteen minutes before outright wishing that Cinderella had died in an alleyway over the course of the night. Kiyara couldn't help but think of her favorite sister as she stood in front of a mirror in her bedroom and stared at herself in the green ballgown. It would not be long before she and her sister flaunted their curves and danced circles around the prince in an effort to do things the easy way. But when Kiyara saw her reflection, all she saw was the demon her mother had turned her into.

She wasn't sure what magic or mental blocks had kept her from processing years of unconscious murder and kidnapping, but whatever she had used to block these thoughts was completely gone. The previous two days had been nothing but a barrage of images, most of them soaked in blood and devastating to her fragile mind.

It took every ounce of self-control not to cry after her mother's new servant had applied a fresh coat of makeup. Her breathing was so quick that she thought she might pass out at any moment.

I have to tell someone what we are. I need somebody to believe what we truly are.... who I am.

As Kiyara looked herself up and down, she thought of Cinderella. She wondered what would happen if the only person in the world who seemed to love her knew the truth about who she was.

"She would have to kill me on the spot, right? It's the only logical thing to do when you find yourself with a monster. You kill it, because otherwise it might murder you and countless others." The tears welled up in her eyes. "And I am a monster."

"You aren't a monster."

Kiyara turned to see her mother at the doorway. She too was dressed in a beautiful gown that enhanced every one of her features. And yet, no matter what her mother wore, she always seemed to be missing something that she had back when they were the rulers of an entire kingdom. It wasn't the crown itself, but Armenia never seemed completely satisfied unless they were the ones on top.

Her mother sat upon her bed and gestured for Kiyara to join her. The young woman hesitated, but eventually she sat.

Armenia sighed. "At first, I didn't realize what I was doing. I thought that by touching you and your sister... by hugging you after I'd sucked out the hearts of men, I assumed I was just making myself feel better. But nothing is ever that simple with magic."

Kiyara had never heard such straight talk from her mother. She leaned in closer to soak up every word.

"The pain and fear allows me entry, but it's the bravery, the valor, the joy that feeds me. It gives me my power, Kiyara. But all the darkness inside of them is too much for me to handle. It's always been too much."

Kiyara sniffled. "So, you didn't mean to turn us into... something horrible?"

Armenia put her hand on her daughter's thigh. "Of course not. I tried everything else to rid myself of the darkness, but the only way to keep it from eating me alive was to share it."

Kiyara let loose a trembling breath. "If you can give it, can you take it all away? Maybe give it all to Malina and let me go back to normal?"

Her mother looked deep into her eyes. A sad smile crept along her lips. "I'm afraid I can't do that, my child."

Kiyara stood up and backed away from her mother. "You're not here to help me. You're here to help yourself."

"I've always given your sister more of the darkness. Much more. I thought you couldn't take the pain, the hate, and the remorse. I thought I was protecting you, but now I know that I was only protecting myself."

Kiyara shook her head and looked toward the room's exit. Her sister stood there like a sentinel.

Kiyara couldn't help it; the tears began to ruin her makeup. "Please, Mother. I can't take any more."

Armenia stood and began to approach. "To stay who you are, you're probably right. But I need to make sure you're on board with the plan. We've decided that this is the only way."

The petrified girl met one of the walls with her back. There was no place else for her to go.

"You're going to lose. The prince won't love me or Malina. We don't deserve another kingdom."

Armenia smirked. "At long last, she displays a backbone. It's too bad you're on the wrong side."

Kiyara could hear her sister laugh as Armenia took the final step and laid her hands on Kiyara's chest. With a wave of energy that rocked her body, she felt the darkness enter. Pain. Hatred. Regret. Anything the woman had left in her body from taking all the feelings of her victims entered into Kiyara's heart.

She cried and cried as she sensed the positivity and goodness being crowded out within her. The waterworks slowed to a trickle as a smile took hold. The blackness coursed through her veins and Kiyara stood up straighter than she had in years.

With the dab of her fingers she wiped away her tears and stepped away from Armenia's touch. She took long, cat-like strides toward the mirror. The girl blew her reflection a kiss and adjusted her dress to emphasize her bosom.

Kiyara turned toward her family. "How on Earth is the prince supposed to resist this?"

Armenia laughed. "Now this is the Kiyara I've always dreamed of having. Welcome."

Malina was in awe, and Kiyara felt herself wanting to slap her sister for the dumbfounded look. She only barely restrained herself.

"I feel better than ever, Mother." She hitched the dress up one more inch. "This kingdom will be ripe for the taking, once you've sucked the prince's grieving heart dry."

PART 4

CHAPTER 31

Cinderella stood atop one of the highest rooftops in the entire village as the evening crept in. It was the only vantage point that gave her a view of her stepmother's house. She'd spent the entire day working the plan over in her mind, but more often than she liked, the thoughts of what her life had truly been crept throughout her consciousness. She stared into her stepmother's window and wondered how much longer she could've not realized the true horrors of her stepmother's misdeeds.

"I know why the Godmother never told me." She clenched and unclenched one of her fists. "I would've had a knife at her throat at the age of ten. But she would've killed me."

The thief let her eyes wander to Malina's window. Not only had the stepsister attempted to torture her every moment they shared in the house, but she was also murdering for Armenia. She had taken part in countless attacks that destroyed families and killed children.

"Not a huge surprise there, but there's a difference between being mean and worshiping evil." The thief let out a heavy breath as her eyes moved to Kiyara's window.

She was the only person in the house who seemed to care for her. Kiyara acted like a true sister, playing with her in the small moments when Armenia turned her back. She was the only one the thief could trust to share the truth with.

"Then why did she hide the truth from me?"

The revelation of her stepmother and Malina being evil did not surprise her all that much. But learning that Kiyara was somehow a part of it all made Cinderella question everything. How long would it be until Kiyara shared all of her secrets with her mother? How long would it be until the girl she considered her true sister killed someone near and dear to the thief?

"I can't hesitate. If I see her, the only right thing to do is to kill her."

Cinderella couldn't bring herself to even think about how she'd raise a sword to Kiyara's neck, but it might be the only way to stop the trio from taking over another kingdom.

She let the carousel of thoughts spin in her head until the carriage pulled around the front of the house. Her stepmother and stepsisters looked incredibly elegant in their gowns. She saw them take the long walk from the door to the carriage, all the while wondering if tonight would be the night she ended their lives. Her eyes focused not on Armenia, who she'd happily dispatch in a moment, but on Kiyara. Her stepsister looked happy as she and Malina held hands. Cinderella could very well attack the carriage now before it made any progress toward the castle, but there was something she still needed to do. As the horses pulled the carriage away, Cinderella's eyes moved up to one last window of the house.

Safely inside, Cinderella paused with her fingers on the doorknob. She couldn't remember the last time she'd been inside this room. Fighting a dozen burly guards didn't make her heart beat as fast as it did in this very moment. She breathed in deeply and turned the handle.

Cinderella stepped into the musty, dry room. It felt like a place where old, unused items were put away in storage, never to be heard from again. She thought the room completely lifeless until she heard a light cough from the bed. Grayer and with more wrinkles than she remembered, her father lay beneath the sheets, his unfeeling eyes fixed upon her.

Every step she took toward the bed felt as if she had heavily weighted shackles on each leg. Snippets of memories from before her mother's death danced across her mind. Nobody would believe it now, but this motionless man beneath the sheets used to play with her. He used to tell her that he loved her. And for so long, Cinderella thought that she had done something unforgivable. That she had somehow caused this man to break and no longer care about her. How many tears had she shed over this painful explanation she'd created for herself?

It took half an age in her mind, but the thief finally reached her father's bedside. The whole time she walked across the room, the man's eyes were locked on her. His face, however, remained otherwise motionless.

She took his weathered hand in hers. "Hello, Father. I don't expect you to listen or love me, but I needed to say something to you before... before Armenia probably kills me too."

A force greater than she'd ever experienced pressed down upon her. It was difficult to breathe. "I know– I know this isn't your fault." She bit her lip to keep the tears at bay. "Damn it. Now I'm going to cry. I'm sure your second wife will really get a kick out of that."

Her father had no reaction to any of the words she said.

She pressed on anyway. "I just had to tell you something." She took in a deep impossible breath. "I don't care what you feel or if you could ever feel something again, but I love you. I love you in this moment, and no magic or evil power can take that away from me. Right now, I love you, Father."

Her father's breath caught for half a moment. Cinderella froze. She leaned in toward him and wondered if there was any chance that he might reciprocate.

But it was just a momentary glitch, and he returned to his steady, motionless, consistent breathing.

She let out the air in her lungs and pressed her lips to his hand. "Goodbye. If I make it, I promise to come back to you and visit your room every single day."

She reluctantly let his hand go and backed toward the door. She let all the pain and insecurity of the last ten years fall away from her and tumble to the ground. It would have to stay here for now.

She took one last look at her father. "I have a job to do."

CHAPTER 32

Prince Braedon couldn't stop his mind from racing down a million different paths. Through his window, he could see all the carriages arriving in the moonlight. He wondered how many women and young girls had bet all their hopes on this night. How many women wanted him to pick them up and transform their lives through his love, his wealth, and his power?

This is a game that has no winners.

He sipped on a small glass of water, which would've been a much stronger drink if his mother had let the quintet of guards in front of his door give him even a sip of booze. He straightened the lapels of his jacket and smoothed the fabric down. There was nothing more he wanted than to rip this outfit from his body, put on a fighting tunic, and dash across the rooftops with Cinderella. With the two of them combined, he knew they could stop this menace once and for all. He pictured the thief's face for a moment before a disruption from the hallway cleared the thoughts from his head. He turned to see a scuffle as someone was trying to enter his chambers.

"What is the meaning of this? I am a knight of the queen's castle and I wish to speak to the prince immediately."

Braedon rolled his eyes. "Let him pass. He means me no harm. Well, not much harm anyway."

Stumbling backward into the room and barely avoiding impaling himself on a lamp, Falstone was dressed in finery that may have fit him properly about five to ten years ago. The seams were stretched so tight, the knight was poised to tear his shirt apart with any movement.

His smile was wide and intoxicated. "My boy. Look at how well you clean up." He whistled loudly. "If I were of a different persuasion, I would have to shower you with affection."

Braedon sighed. "I'm touched, Falstone. But please don't talk about showering me with affection."

The hefty knight slapped the prince on the shoulder. "Have I told you lately that you are like a son to me?"

The prince looked up at the man's bearded face. "You can't have it both ways. You can't say that I'm attractive and also your son."

Falstone's laughter echoed through the prince's chambers. "They've kept you sober too long, my friend. Your wit is getting almost too fast for old Don Falstone to understand it."

The knight looked around in every direction. "Where are the drinks? I thought you'd be celebrating your night among the ladies."

The prince gestured with his chin toward the guards at the door. "My mother's welcome wagon isn't very interested in letting me imbibe today."

Falstone returned an incredulous look. "I've never heard of a worse atrocity in all my life. And I was married three times!"

The prince pointed toward his dresser. "You can have all the tea you like. In the last day I've had more tea than my body can handle."

The large knight wrinkled his face but stepped up to the makeshift bar anyway. He poured himself a small glass of brown, pungent liquid, and revealed a flask from his pocket. He expertly concealed it from the guards' view, helped himself to a mighty portion, and stowed it back in his trousers. He took a sip and smiled. "Not half bad with the right extra ingredients." He raised an eyebrow. "How goes our demon problem?"

The prince shook his head. "I haven't been allowed to investigate, so Cinderella has probably had to do it all on her own."

He squinted. "You still haven't gotten over her yet?"

"It's been a day, Falstone."

"Exactly. You are about to have dozens of women fawning over you." Falstone tried to mimic a waltz as he walked over, but he just looked like his body was twitching uncontrollably. "If these beautiful vixens smell even a hint of love for another woman on you, you have little to no chance to bring them back up here."

The prince balled up his fist and knocked his knuckles on Falstone's head. "I'm not interested in them. I don't even know if I'm fully interested in Elle, but I need to get in touch with her." He looked over at the guards by the door. None of them were paying full attention to him and Falstone. He ran over to a small table and began scrawling something on a piece of parchment. "I have a mission for you, Falstone. Secret, royal business."

The knight's smile grew wide. "My favorite kind of business. What do you need me to do? Drink a foreign dignitary under the table? I'd be great at that."

The prince finished his message and held it up in the air. After checking it over one more time, he nodded his approval and folded it up. "You're always intercepting my messages. I'd like you to deliver one, instead."

Falstone nodded. "I can do that. I can certainly do that, my boy. It's about time you trusted me with some secret royal business."

The prince handed over the message, which Falstone promptly put into his flask pocket. "Find Cinderella and deliver this to her."

He raised an eyebrow. "Wait. You want me to leave the ball? I had plans for this. I've got my eye on a vintage brandy and several vintage widows."

Braedon put his hand on Falstone's shoulder. "Don't worry, you'll have plenty of time to come back and get the party going when you return. The... drinks will still be here."

"Very well. In the name of the Prince of Loren, I will fulfill this duty for you. But you may need to give me some more tea on the way out. This is actually quite good."

Braedon patted his heavyset friend on the shoulder. "That's the spirit. You can have all the tea you want."

Falstone surprised the prince by spinning toward him and giving him a massive bear hug.

The prince struggled to breathe in his friend's massive grasp.

"I'm proud of you, my boy. Your father would be, too."

Braedon coughed. "Thanks– Falstone– can you– it's a tight hug–"

The knight released him and grinned. "I just have too much love to give, I suppose. I'll make sure this message gets into the right hands."

Braedon let as much oxygen as possible into his lungs. "I appreciate that. Goodbye, old friend."

Falstone dashed over to the dresser, filled his cup halfway with tea, and topped the rest off with his special concoction. "And goodbye to you, Your

Royal Highness." He took a large gulp. "Ahhh. The sweet taste of secrets." Then he lumbered out of the room and past the group of guards.

The prince chuckled to himself. "If that message ever sees the light of day, it'll be a miracle." A flickering light caught the prince's eyes from just outside the window. "Now what the heck is that?"

Braedon stepped toward the clear glass before him and saw that what glimmered wasn't just a light, it was gold. A bird he couldn't help but recognize flapped its wings and stared right at him. But that wasn't even the most interesting part. The bird appeared to be wearing something around its neck that dangled all the way beneath its feet. The prince had a sneaking suspicion that whatever this object was, it was meant for him.

CHAPTER 33

Cinderella prepared for the ball by sharpening her weapons.

She loved the sound of stone on metal and the sparks that shot into the air when she moved her blade at just the right angle. Part of her wished she could stay in preparation mode all night long, but tonight would be a confrontation ten years in the making. She felt a presence behind her and turned to see the Godmother staring down at her.

The thief blew metal shavings off a dagger as she placed it into the third scabbard on her belt. "I think I'm ready for this. All the weapons are in good condition, and I believe I have a strong plan of entry. Did you need anything?"

The Godmother beamed with pride. "You really have turned into quite the young woman."

The thief wasn't sure exactly how to react. Her forehead creased. "Is this about the twins telling me everything? I know you had your reasons for not being forthcoming, so you don't need to get all weepy on me."

"I don't plan on crying; it's just an observation. You're strong, you're smart, and the prince wasn't able to take his eyes off you the second he saw your face. I would have to say that you are a very impressive young woman."

Cinderella grunted. "If this is your idea of a pep talk, I'm not sure it's working."

The Godmother stepped into the light. "I'm sorry that I didn't tell you more, sooner. You learned what you needed to learn in the exact order it came. But that doesn't mean it was easy for you, or that it was right of me to withhold that information."

The thief stood up. When she first entered the care of her mentor, she would have to look almost straight up to meet her eyes. Now, they were nearly the same height.

"Why did you take me in all those years ago? Was it just to stop Armenia when she rose to power, or was there something else behind it?"

They heard a small child's grunt from the other room, followed by several whaps against a burlap sack. Hannah was already training to be just like the thief.

The Godmother searched for the right words. "People who have had a horrible tragedy in their lives tend to gravitate toward one another. It's only when pain is shared that it can be turned into something so much greater."

Cinderella huffed. "I'm not so sure about that."

"Prince Braedon might have a different idea than you do."

The thief gave a sharp chuckle and turned around. "The prince abandoned me. We had a chance to take this on together, but he decided he had to go through official channels. If I had any momentary... feelings for him, his little act of treason surely snuffed them out."

Her mentor laughed. It was so rare for Cinderella to hear mirth from her caretaker that her chest began to warm.

The Godmother looked wise as she smiled. "It's never that simple, Elle. If we expect everybody in our lives to be perfect all of the time then we will most surely be alone. But you are not alone, and I have a bit of evidence to prove it."

From behind her back the Godmother revealed a glowing golden dress. It was the most incredible thing she had ever seen. The thief had spied countless dresses paraded before her by Malina and her stepmother, but she wasn't sure anybody had laid eyes on an outfit quite like this.

The thief's voice hitched. "I was planning on sneaking in."

The Godmother walked closer and gestured with her eyes for Cinderella to touch the dress. When she did, she could feel just how silky and smooth it was. It also smelled incredible, as if it belonged at the ball.

Her mentor cradled the dress like an infant. "The twins spun this dress themselves in repayment for you saving their lives."

The thief looked up. "How am I going to–"

"Don't worry, it has hidden weapon holsters built in."

Cinderella laughed. "I guess they know me after all." Her hands paused above the dress for a moment until she finally decided to take what was hers. She grabbed the golden garment and prepared to change into it.

Before she could, the Godmother took her by the shoulder. "I need you to remember something, Elle."

The thief nodded.

"Revenge is about hate and anger. If you go into this to help other people, and if you think nothing of yourself in the process, then you may be able to take a much more positive, loving approach. Trust me when I say, it's a lot more fulfilling than revenge."

Cinderella looked between her mentor's eyes and the dress. She let her teeth press into the inside of her cheek. "Dammit, everything is going to make me cry today." She grabbed the Godmother in a tight hug and didn't want to let go. Her mentor held her back in a moment the thief didn't want to end. When she finally let go, Cinderella didn't hesitate on her path to the next room.

When she was alone again, she looked at the dress not like an object of clothing, but like a partner on her most important mission.

"All right, dress. Let's see exactly what kind of damage we can do."

CHAPTER 34

Beset by bright, shining colors and decadent foods all around her, Kiyara could feel a dark war raging inside. As she smiled and twirled next to her sister Malina, she could sense all the pain, anguish, and grief that her mother had channeled into her on one side of her mind. On the other side cowered the goodness and love that desperately clung to her soul. On the inside, she knew which side was the real her, but it was trapped in a mental prison.

She no longer looked at her sister as one of the scariest people she knew, but as a rival for the prince's affection. When she laughed with incredible confidence, she was fixated on how the other women at the party looked at her with envy. It made the new additions to her personality crave the adoration and jealousy of others. It was a feeling that was completely insatiable. As her spine stood straighter than it had ever been, Kiyara moved to the music of the violin and saw Prince Braedon from across the room.

The timid parts of her that remained on lockdown were absolutely terrified. They compelled Kiyara to step away and hide herself among the gathering's wallflowers. Instead, she stuck out her chest and strode in a straight line toward her prey. She could feel her mouth curl in a smile that was nearly too perfect to be believed. She watched the prince dance with another woman. She had dark hair and looked about the same age as Kiyara and her sister. To the new, darker parts of Kiyara, the girl was nothing but a rival to be torn down and thrown to the wolves. While a small part of her could detect the deadness in the prince's eyes, the majority in control chose to ignore that fact.

She expertly spun close enough to the prince's dance partner to smell the girl's skin. With one twirl, a sharp diamond from one of the rings her mother had given her made contact at the exact right moment with one of the straps of the girl's dress. Nobody saw that Kiyara was the cause of the garment tearing apart. The girl shrieked so loud it pulled Braedon out of his stupor. He jumped back as his brunette partner clutched at her dress and turned red. She walked away in utter embarrassment, with partygoers laughing and gasping at her.

One down. A few dozen to go.

Kiyara twirled until her hands were in the prince's. He was shocked by the quick switch, until he recognized the girl before him.

"Kiyara. Thank the gods. Someone who probably wants to be here just as little as me."

She smiled an immaculate smile and pulled herself closer to him. "I can't believe you remembered me. I was a mess at that party."

The prince backed away slightly to provide a bit more space between them. "You were real." His eyes scanned the rest of the crowd. "You weren't hiding your emotions like most of these people. Some of them are even betting their lives on being able to romance me."

Kiyara let out a flighty laugh, a sound that had never before exited her mouth. "Romancing doesn't sound so bad, with the right person."

Braedon turned his attention back toward her. He had a confused look on his face. "You seem different. Are you okay?"

Kiyara wanted to press herself into him and take him away from all of these awful people, her sister included. She also knew in the darkest parts of her that she deserved to be the future queen.

"Everything has changed. I'm not the girl who cried all over you just a few days ago." Her fingers pressed into him. "I'm a woman who's willing to take what she's earned."

The prince started to let her hand go. "You don't need to be different. Seeing your emotions open up like that made me know who you really are."

Undeterred, Kiyara tightened her grasp on the prince. "This is who I am. The girl you saw in the garden is gone forever."

The prince wrenched himself free of her and politely moved to the side. He shook his head. "It's a shame you felt the need to change. Showing who you really were was all that made you stand apart from your sister. All that made you stand apart from everybody else here. Excuse me."

She watched the prince's back as he left. After the wave of confusion subsided, hate and anger bubbled to the surface. She looked down at her dainty, pale hand, and saw the sharp metallic claws begin to extract themselves from her fingers. She was about to let them all the way out in the midst of the crowd, when Armenia took her hand and begin to soothingly rub the palm.

"My dear, dear girl. He doesn't understand who we are and why we must be loved."

Kiyara couldn't let the rage subside so quickly. "He said I was better before. He said I wasn't being real anymore."

Her mother hushed her. As she continued to stroke her palm, the claws retracted back into her human fingers. "His poor judgment of your character will be the beginning of his downfall. Failure to choose either you or your sister has made quite a different choice for him indeed. Tonight is when it ends. Tonight is when we reclaim all that we deserve."

The silent part within Kiyara screamed and pounded to get out. It was no use.

The dominant persona smiled at the thought of retribution. "I feel like I should already start calling you queen."

The glow of a burning ember lit up Armenia's eye. "Soon enough, Princess. Soon enough."

Kiyara noticed several guests around her turn their attention to the top of a tall marble staircase at the other side of the room. She watched her mother's eyes stare in a curious manner in the same direction. She followed the path to the topmost step, and her jaw began to drop. A graceful, golden young woman with matching glass shoes took her first step toward the party. The dress was truly captivating, and Kiyara wondered how easily she could kill her own dressmaker for failing to match the sheer beauty of the outfit she saw walking toward them. Even the music stopped when the girl reached the halfway point, her eyes fixed forward into the middle of the crowd.

Several waves of realization hit Kiyara all at once. The first was that the woman in gold wasn't merely looking at just any point in the gaggle of guests. Her eyes were locked upon Prince Braedon's. The second was that the man with whom she'd just been dancing, who had shunned her embarrassingly, was looking right back. But it was the third point that stung her the most. It was the moment she finally realized that the girl was her lowly stepsister, Cinderella.

The room was so quiet, Kiyara could hear the individual breaths of the people throughout the room. She wanted to end their unimportant lives, along with the lives of both Braedon and Cinderella.

She knew that within the hour, she would have a chance to destroy them all.

CHAPTER 35

Prince Braedon forgot how to breathe. For a moment, he'd forgotten how to walk and talk as well. The only thing his body would allow him to do was to stare slightly upward to see Cinderella descending her way back into his life. Even though her attire was a far cry from her thieving cloaks, which in his opinion looked pretty good to begin with, he knew her the moment the rest of the party turned in her direction. When her eyes connected with his across the room, Braedon felt as though the entire ballroom had frozen. As if they were the only ones there.

He wished that everyone around them would magically vanish, because being alone with her in this moment would be pure perfection. His mother had once told him that she hoped he could find both the perfect partner and someone to fall in love with. He wasn't sure if love was the combination of the fast heartbeat and locked brain that he experienced right now, but the sensation was certainly something new.

The prince wasn't sure what guided his feet to the base of the staircase, but he was there when the golden woman of his dreams reached the final step. He took her hand and guided her to the middle of the dance floor, where the rest of the crowd had created a path for them to travel. Cinderella waited until the partygoers around them formed a bit of a bubble around the two before she finally spoke.

Her eyes were locked on his. "I'm not sure how your other guests wear this stuff. It gets a lot of attention. I'm not really used to attention."

Braedon looked left and right and saw that nearly every eye in the ballroom was on them. He glanced up to the likewise staring musicians and cleared his throat.

As if shaken from a trance, the players began their music once again with a slow waltz. The prince placed his hand on the thief's lower back and gently brought her to him. Touching the dress and being so close to her shot a wave of energy through his entire body.

Braedon laughed. "There certainly are more people in here than you'd find on most rooftops. Where did you get that dress?"

Her eyes drooped down and looked at her outfit before coming back to his. "I have a feeling that if I told you, you wouldn't believe me."

The prince felt his cheeks redden. "Over the last few days, I've realized I should believe everything you say."

"And I have a feeling if you did, I would take complete advantage of you."

For the first time that evening, the prince let the heavy weight off his chest. "I'm sorry. I messed up, and then the queen wouldn't let me leave. I should've been there to help and I feel wretched for– for skipping out on you at a very important time."

The thief smirked. "You know, it's not like I haven't worked alone for a very long time. I took care of myself."

"Of course. I know that. But I don't want you to have to. You deserve an equal partner. I think maybe I could be that–"

"There she is! I have a note for you, little lady."

Both Braedon and Cinderella turned their heads at the very same moment to see a bumbling knight stomp his way toward them.

The prince's cheeks grew warmer. "Falstone! You were supposed to find her before–"

He laughed and placed his hands on both of their backs at once. "I know, I know. I got caught up with a few old friends. But now, I have the opportunity to make a new one." He pulled Cinderella's hand from the prince's grasp and brought it up to his mouth. "Charmed to meet you, my lady."

As the sweaty knight brought her hand to his lips, the thief had her eyebrows raised and pointed in Braedon's direction the entire time. After Falstone held her hand for an uncomfortably long period of time, Cinderella withdrew it as politely as she could.

"Sir Falstone, I've heard far too much about you to kiss you back."

The man's cheeks turned as red as Braedon's as he howled with laughter, sending even more eyes toward them. "My boy, it's no wonder that you're crazy about her."

Braedon wasn't sure his face could get any hotter.

The thief smirked. "Crazy about me, eh? Can you tell me a little bit more?"

The prince stammered. "I– he meant to say… I think I need to go outside."

Before Cinderella could respond, a shriek pierced through the music. Braedon turned toward the noise and saw something that made his blood run cold. Standing beside his mother were two grotesque demons. Their claws were wrapped around her dress, poised to strike and spill her blood at a moment's notice.

CHAPTER 36

Cinderella didn't hesitate for a second. As soon as she saw the two creatures that were somehow her own stepsisters, she reached into the folds of her dress and pulled out a dagger. She used it to snip off a few threads that connected to a long, flowing part of her dress. The material fell to the floor, leaving Cinderella's legs free for combat. All around the room, women and men alike screamed at the sight of the demons, and about a dozen guards sprung into action. Unfortunately for them, approximately half of their ranks were apparently on Armenia's side. The unluckiest among the Queen's Guard received a sword in the back. It was utter chaos.

The prince's head darted from side to side to try to keep track of it all. He saw the nearest sword from one of the fallen guards and made a run for it. Cinderella caught his arm before he could take a single step.

Braedon growled. "I need to stop them from killing her."

Cinderella's eyes fought to grab his attention. "Don't think about her right now. We will save her, but we need to get through these guards first. Focus will keep you from getting knifed."

Even amid the wild screaming and dashing around them, the prince nodded his understanding.

The thief nodded back and let him go toward the sword. She had enough time to glance up to see the demons scurrying the queen off to another room. She was not surprised to see Armenia behind the trio, a glowing red fireball in her right hand.

"I hope we'll all have our vengeance tonight."

Cinderella kicked off her glass slippers and went running for one of the turncoats. One of Armenia's men laughed when he saw her coming, which gave the thief just enough time to slice his wrist to lower his sword hand

and kick him right in the throat with the ball of her foot. Two additional fake guards approached her. Before she could plot her attack, the prince held a new weapon and stood by her side.

He winked. "Shall we let the real dance begin?"

The thief licked her lips. "I lead."

"Wouldn't have it any other way."

When the guards were but a few feet away, Braedon and the thief easily rolled beneath their swinging swords. Braedon whipped his weapon back around and slammed the attacker in the head with it, while Cinderella spun her legs back and heard a crack from the back of the other turncoat's kneecap. Both of Armenia's men crumpled to the ground in pain.

Cinderella and the prince only had a moment to smile, before she saw a man approaching behind his shoulder. "Duck."

The prince complied, bending at the waist while the thief dove over him with her legs extended. The man had no chance to draw his weapon as she kicked him so hard in the sternum that he lost his balance completely. The spy slammed his back on one of the hard wooden tables and clutched it as he fell down.

When she turned back toward her dance partner, she watched him easily avoid half a dozen swipes with a sword using his newly enhanced agility. With moves so quick she could barely make them out, he used his own weapon to knock the sword out of the spy's hand before he roundhouse-kicked the man's nose, bending it sideways and causing it to spill out blood.

The thief rushed to his side. "You're quick."

"You should see my tango." He pointed to the other side of the room. "Will you look at that?"

Cinderella watched with a smile as the drunken knight Falstone swung a leg he must've ripped off a table into the heads of two unsuspecting spies. Falstone screamed in victory after knocking them both out.

Cinderella shrugged. "Never get between a man and his party."

She watched the prince's eyes shoot upward to the place the queen had previously been standing. "They're headed to the throne room. We need to move quickly."

Cinderella nodded, and they dashed up the staircase together. The prince and the thief easily dispatched the trio of guards that stood between them and the royal hostage. Cinderella used momentum to toss a couple of them over the railing, while Braedon's speed was too much for the third one to handle. She could still hear his string of curses tumbling down the stairs as they reached the second-floor hallway. The prince waved her ahead and they sprinted toward the sound of two gurgling monsters and their fiery leader.

She'd never seen Braedon look so serious.

"If they harm a single hair on her head–"

She stowed her dagger in mid-stride and prepared to reach for the jeweled sword. "She's going to be fine, Braedon. I'll make sure of that."

Braedon stopped them at the beginning of a short hallway lined with ornate decorations and paintings. The thief had no time to admire the beauty, as there were six more guards standing between them and their objective. They all wore thick armor and were starting to move toward them.

Cinderella grinned. "You go low, I'll go high."

The prince returned a smile and prepared his weapon. That's when the thief began sprinting.

Cinderella waited until exactly the right moment to take flight. The outstretched swords of the heavily armored men merely grazed her dress as she leapt high into the air. All six of Armenia's guards watched her as she somersaulted through the air. The thief made her best effort to hover as long as possible. She didn't even need to look to know that Braedon would have all the opportunity he needed.

Cinderella heard the Prince of Loren run at top speed with his weapon drawn. Braedon blazed through a half-dozen spies with the side of his sword, easily tripping all of the men with his incredible momentum. They yelped, and shouted, and cursed, as the armor that made them nearly invulnerable became their downfall as well.

Cinderella landed on the other side of the now-harmless knights. The prince took a leap of his own and landed beside her. She smiled at the sight of the pinned men, who reminded her of turtles stuck on their backs.

Braedon raised his eyebrows. "That was a nice plan, Elle."

"Speed trumps armor. Let's save your mom."

Braedon nodded and they rushed through the open hallway into the throne room. The room was just as intricately decorated as the hallway had been. Paintings and jewelry from every corner of the world covered the walls and ceilings above. Cinderella thought it was no wonder that the queen had been after the Heartstone. It probably would have gone on one of the corners of the window. But Cinderella didn't have much time to admire the artwork.

She could see plainly as day that her two demon stepsisters continued to hold the queen hostage. That didn't surprise her, but the thing that did was that Armenia herself sat upon the throne. A throne that was covered from top to bottom in terrifying flames.

CHAPTER 37

All the feelings of excitement and strength that accompanied the prince as he fought with Cinderella by his side evaporated as soon as he saw his mother up close. One of the beasts had already punctured her skin with its claws, and a thin trickle of red blood spilled down the front of her dress. His mother was the most incredible, strong woman he'd ever seen. He hadn't even been sure she could bleed until now.

He spoke more assertively than he felt. "Unhand my mother, Armenia. This isn't a fight you can win."

Armenia grinned and crossed her legs. "Oh really? I think I have all the power in this situation. And all you have is idle chatter." She looked at her flaming throne and then back over to him. "I even have the throne. I think it's possible I've already won."

While the prince held his ground, he could feel Cinderella moving toward his mother.

Armenia held up her hand. "Tut-tut, daughter. I think you've gotten close enough."

The prince was surprised when he saw that Cinderella didn't even look up at her evil stepmother. She focused right in on one of the demons.

He was even more shocked by the name she used.

"Kiyara, you don't have to do this. I know that she's forcing you to do it."

One of the two demons who held his mother in check hissed loudly. She even began to form words. "You don't know me, slave girl. This is who I am now."

Cinderella's face showed pure resolve. "No, it's not. I know you better than them. I know you better than anybody else in this world."

147

The prince now understood why he recognized the eyes of the demon he'd faced. It had been Malina. And the other demon was her sister, Kiyara. He wasn't sure how it made sense, but it did.

Braedon shook off his confusion and looked into the eyes of his mother. "It's okay, Mother. We're going to get you out of this."

The queen's skin started to look pale. "I'm proud of you, Braedon. Maybe not the boozing, but I'm generally proud."

"Don't you go saying goodbye right now!"

Armenia's laughter echoed throughout the chamber as she stood up and stretched. The witch made it look as if it was part of her throne room routine.

She stepped down toward them. "It is time for many goodbyes, Prince Braedon. Of course, you should start to say goodbye to your mother. You should also bid farewell to the kingdom you once knew. Loren will be a very different place without your mother. Without the essence of who you are."

Cinderella and the prince both took a step back with every pace she took.

Braedon held his sword up high. "That's enough, Armenia. Make this between you and me, and leave my mother out of this."

Armenia continued to walk forward. Each stride felt like a dagger scraping against his skin.

"Part of me is glad that I was banished. I had grown weak and predictable. My daughters were maturing in a life of pure luxury." She smiled widely at Cinderella. "It was time for a change of scenery. It was time to steal someone else's life."

The prince could see how much the thief was fighting her desire to take a stab at revenge. He figured that she knew as well as he did that the numbers and the power were not on their side.

Cinderella breathed heavily. "Kiyara, you need to help me. You know the queen and the prince have done nothing wrong. This is your opportunity to show them who you really are. To show them you are the sister I love."

The demon-form of Kiyara relinquished her grasp on the queen and held her clawed hands up to the sides of her head. "Enough, servant. Stop talking right now!"

"We're not related by blood, Kiyara, but you are my sister."

Kiyara grunted. "Leave me alone!"

Armenia continued to step toward them. "It's no use, Stepdaughter. You may confuse her for a while, but she will always come back to her mother. It's too bad that you aren't able to do the same. I really should have made sure that I burned you to death like I did your mother."

The prince turned toward the thief. He watched Cinderella grit her teeth and fight with everything she had not to give in.

He reached toward her. "She's just trying to rile you up. Everything is going to be okay."

Cinderella was so angry that she couldn't even speak.

Braedon spun back toward the queen. "You're right, Armenia. You have all the power in this situation. You're the one in charge."

The evil fiery witch stopped in her tracks, sneering. "I'm glad you're finally willing to acknowledge this, Your Royal Highness."

Braedon laid down his sword and took a step in her direction. "We don't have to fight. I'm sure my mother and I will be willing to abdicate the throne to you as long as you spare us our lives."

The queen moaned in Malina's grasp. "Don't, Braedon. Don't give in."

Her demon captor laughed. "Quiet. You no longer have importance."

The prince moved ahead once again. "Armenia, I'm telling you that you can have everything you want."

Armenia's grin was pure evil incarnate. "But the only thing I truly want, dear Prince, is your heart."

Time seemed to freeze as Armenia nodded to her daughter. Braedon and the thief both dashed toward the queen, but it was too late. With the stab of her claws through the regent's back, Malina took the queen's life. The prince felt his limbs fall motionless by his sides as he watched his mother drop to the ground, lifeless. He heard Cinderella shout something as she drew her sword, but even as time moved slowly, Armenia was far too fast for any of them. In a magical blaze of light, the witch had wrenched Braedon from his statue-like state and yanked him toward the throne. He felt himself being pulled through the air in a world where he no longer had control.

Armenia tossed the new ruler of Loren into his throne and placed her hand on his chest. Everything he ever knew and loved and hated drained out of him, and the scream that left his mouth was the last thing he remembered.

CHAPTER 38

Cinderella couldn't believe it. The sequence of events that had seen the queen fall dead and Prince Braedon pulled from her grasp was the worst-case scenario by far. Despite drawing the Heartstone sword, Armenia continued to pull life from the prince's body. Cinderella let out a war cry and ran toward her stepmother.

Red flames shot through Armenia's eyes as she tossed a ball of flame toward the thief. Cinderella rolled to the side to avoid it. She continued running. Armenia threw another fireball, this one larger than the first. Cinderella rolled and ducked and kept on sprinting.

As Armenia kept working Braedon over, she threw a third, carriage-sized fiery blast in the thief's direction. With no chance to avoid it, Cinderella tightened her grasp on the sword's hilt and the fiery death was averted. The fireball dissipated before it could reach her.

Cinderella growled. "Let him go, or I swear–"

Malina tackled her stepsister and clawed at her face. Cinderella's back landed hard on the stone ground, knocking most of the wind out of her. As she struggled to breathe, the sword was the only thing that prevented an immediate mauling. Malina's demon body pressed down hard on the thief's chest. She was too heavy to shake off, and Cinderella's best efforts to roll were for naught.

She glanced sideways for a moment to see Armenia standing over a dead-eyed Braedon. Anger and remorse went through every part of her body, giving her the strength she needed to push the massive creature off her. Malina flew back and landed with a thump. When Cinderella looked up, she saw the prince standing. She knew the look in his face immediately. The man she knew was gone. Like her father and the blacksmith before him, he would never feel anything again.

As much as she hated to do it, she turned her attention away from mourning and toward winning the battle. Her eyes leapt towards Kiyara, who stood over the dead queen's body.

Her voice quivered. "If you feel remorse, my sister, it means that is the real you. It doesn't matter what your mother made you into. What you choose to do is who you are." The thief screamed the final words. "So do something about it!"

Kiyara got the message. With a primal yell, Cinderella's sister dashed across the room and attacked Malina. She watched the demons grappling for position, a mass of gray muscle and bone.

The thief stepped toward the throne, which now featured a lifeless prince standing before it. To the side was her stepmother, just asking for an opportunity to exact revenge upon her.

The thief seethed with anger and stepped toward the witch, but her stepmother was no longer the size she remembered.

Flames started to spill their way down her body, as Armenia laughed. "His heart was so delicious. Never tasted anything like–"

Armenia yelled with power as her body started to grow even bigger. She quickly passed the demonic size of her daughters as the red and orange flames continued to lick her body. She was becoming massive, but Cinderella held strong.

"I will not let you intimidate me, Mother."

Armenia's voice boomed. "It doesn't matter if you're scared. You'll die either way."

A deep, unsteady voice entered the fray. "Nobody does that to my boy!"

Cinderella turned to see Falstone running forward and tossing a full bottle of pure alcohol directly into Armenia's face. The spirits caught fire and gave a flash of light. Unfortunately, Armenia seemed unfazed by the momentary light show.

"Stupid fool." She threw a fireball in Falstone's direction. The thief rushed over and made the projectile fizzle before it could sear the large knight to death.

Cinderella pulled Falstone behind the base of a massive sculpture.

Armenia's laughter continued to echo through the room.

The thief looked over and saw Kiyara fighting blow for blow with her sister. Their demonic shrieks were loud and would have been terrifying to most.

Cinderella looked back to Falstone. "You need to get out of here. It isn't safe for you."

"I'm not leaving him."

She took him by the shoulders. "He's gone, Falstone. He's like the others. He's gone."

As the realization hit the inebriated Falstone, it trickled through the thief as well. The man she trained with. The man who leapt from rooftop to rooftop with her. He would never return. All that remained was the same husk of a person that her father and Tristan and all those soldiers had become.

She fought off the darkness and tried to internalize what the Godmother had told her earlier. This wasn't about her anymore.

"Just stay here in the corner."

Falstone nodded and crouched by the wall. She didn't want to see the pain in his eyes.

The thief stepped out from behind the sculpture and held her sword high. "Mother, if you want to take this kingdom, you're going to have to go through me first."

The gargantuan Armenia ceased her laughing. "Gladly."

As Cinderella expected, her giant stepmother's motions were slower. It was easy for the thief to watch Armenia's movements toward her and estimate her timing. There would be no more surprises.

Cinderella could feel the heat from her stepmother's flaming body. But the raging flames that extended far beyond the witch's reach met a protective bubble around the thief. The sword was doing its work.

Cinderella prepared to strike. At the moment Armenia swung a large and fiery fist toward the thief, Cinderella swung her sword as well. As the blade and hand met, a blast of energy shot in every direction, sending sparks and the light skyward. The thief and the blade held their ground against the much larger witch. Armenia growled and pressed her hand into the sword, but the thief would not yield. At a stalemate, Cinderella pressed her stepmother back and did a series of backward flips to put some distance between them. Cinderella caught a glimpse of Malina on top of Kiyara, trying to claw caverns into her body. She also looked over at the motionless prince.

It's all going to hell.

Armenia screamed and dashed across the room toward her adversary. With expert timing, the thief leapt above the outstretched hand of her stepmother and swung down upon the fiery shoulder. Armenia cried out in pain, but there was no blood. The fire she momentarily extinguished came right back afterwards. Cinderella landed and rolled to the side to avoid a fiery projectile.

Armenia cackled once again. "I've grown too powerful for that stone to have an effect on me anymore. The fight is lost, little girl."

Cinderella went for one last rush at Armenia's legs, but the giant flaming creature swung her hands so quickly, she didn't have time to react. The attack burned her hands and caused her to drop the Heartstone sword. Armenia let the flames on her right hand dissipate as she grabbed the thief by the neck and hoisted her high into the air. Cinderella felt her throat constrict as she attempted unsuccessfully to let the air pass through. As she swung her legs wildly, she spied her sister on the ground. No longer in the form of a demon, Kiyara had reverted to human form. And she wasn't breathing.

The thief squealed and kicked and did everything she could to get out of the creature's grasp. It was no use.

Armenia had joy in her eyes. "The sister you love is dead. The mother you loved is dead. And neither your father nor your beloved prince will ever remember you again."

The thief did everything she could to shut out the emotional daggers that sliced at her heart. She fought hard to remember exactly what the Godmother had said.

Armenia moved her giant hand down Cinderella's body, allowing the thief to breathe once more. With all her stepmother's might, she pressed Cinderella against the wall and placed her palm over the thief's chest.

"Now let's take a look inside that grief-stricken heart of yours."

Armenia pushed into Cinderella's body and began to draw out everything from her heart. The thief's world went black.

CHAPTER 39

Cinderella's eyes opened wide. She still saw flames to the left and the right, but she was no longer pinned against the wall in a massive, decadent throne room. She couldn't see the dead-eyed prince or her deceased sister anywhere. Even Armenia had vanished from her view. All she saw was a room that she'd memorized every corner of. Every wall and every flame was familiar, because it was the room where her mother had died. In the familiar spot, Cinderella saw the body of her mother. But something was different about all of it. The flames usually let off so much heat that it made the thief sweat in her sleep. But she didn't feel anything. In fact, something about the flames and smoke around her made her feel almost stronger.

"What is this place?"

When nothing answered, she walked toward her mother. The flames around her continued to have no effect. She noticed that in her dreams she would often have the body of a child… the child who watched her mother die. And yet, she was her exact right age in this place. She wore her typical black thieving cloak and could feel the Heartstone sword in her scabbard. Whatever realm she'd stumbled into, it certainly wasn't the same old dream.

Cinderella knelt beside her mother. She looked over to the side of the room that in recent nights had featured the golden bird leading her into safety. That's when she realized that the bird was standing beside her. Not in its typical form, but as the little golden child. Cinderella blinked and saw that both twins were standing beside her.

Cinderella pursed her lips. "Aymee. Tressa. What is this place?"

The twins smiled in unison before Aymee opened her mouth. "Your mother is ready to speak to you now."

Cinderella's hand absently rubbed her thigh. "Am I dead? Am I with my mother?"

Tressa let out a giggle. "Just talk to her. It's why you're here."

Cinderella pulled her focus from the golden twins and let her hand lightly touch her mother's shoulder. She expected it to be cold and dead. But she was overwhelmed when she realized this woman beneath her had a pulse. She was very much alive.

Cinderella's chest tightened. "Mother?" She lightly shook the shoulder. "Mother?"

The thief's mother turned toward her, but she did not wear the face Cinderella remembered. The woman didn't seem to be her mother at all.

It was her mentor. The Godmother.

Cinderella forced herself to breathe. "What's happening here? I don't understand."

The Godmother smiled and took her fingers. "I think you do. I think if you search deep down, you do."

Cinderella's heart opened wide. The Godmother had looked different. Had acted different. Even though it seemed absolutely impossible, her mentor had the spirit of her mother with her all along. Somehow, the woman who'd guided her all these years was actually her mother.

She held her breath and intertwined their fingers. "Why didn't you tell me? How did I not know? How did you find a way to reach me?"

The Godmother sat up and wrapped her arms around Cinderella. The thief felt herself sink into her mother's touch for the first time in a decade. It was like coming home.

Her mentor squeezed tight. "Not every question needs an answer, but you don't need to die today like I died so many years ago."

Cinderella pulled back to look her mentor in the eye. To look her mother in the eye. "I'm not dead? I can still win this fight?"

"I may have trained you to be strong. To be fast. To be resilient. But you always had the thing you needed to defeat your greatest enemy."

Through all the unanswered questions Cinderella had had over the last decade, this was one she was able to answer herself right away. She nodded and smiled.

The Godmother let her hands slip down to meet Cinderella's. "It's time for you to go."

Cinderella knew that this was true. She sighed. "Will I ever see you again?"

"I'm not sure. But I'll do my best to stay in your thoughts."

Cinderella didn't want to ever leave this place, but she knew she couldn't live in this strange world forever. A single tear rolled down her cheek and made contact with the wood below. She gripped the Godmother's hands and smiled as the vision began to fade away.

The thief's eyes opened once again. This time she was back in the throne room, but now she was on the ground. She looked up to see Armenia in unparalleled distress. Her stepmother's shrieks seemed to rattle the stone walls.

Armenia's screams were so loud and full of pain, Cinderella wondered if the fire on the outside of her body had finally gotten into her veins for the first time. The gigantic woman started to shrink and lose her fiery exterior. By the time the thief had reoriented herself and got to standing, the witch was back to normal size. Her stepmother gritted her teeth and pointed all her ire toward Cinderella.

She balled up both of her fists. "How? How were you able to resist me?"

At the very same moment, the thief and her stepmother both spied the Heartstone sword from across the room. Without hesitation, both of them ran for it. Armenia was quick, but Cinderella had something else working for her. As she grew closer to the weapon, she rolled forward, picked up the sword in one motion, and held the jeweled part of the blade up to her chest. "How did I resist? My love is stronger than your hate."

The second the jewel made contact with the area above the thief's heart, a light brighter than anything she had ever seen radiated out from it. Cinderella squinted against a light as powerful as the sun, which fired a constant beam across the throne room and directly into her stepmother's chest. The screams before were no match for the sounds that came out of Armenia's mouth just then.

Deep, dark, guttural sounds bounced against the walls of the throne room as Armenia twitched within the throes of the light. Cinderella watched with some difficulty through the brightness as her stepmother's body began to cave in on itself. The screams continued until the proud, heartless woman blinked out of existence, leaving nothing but a faint wisp of smoke behind. The light from the sword extinguished itself, and the thief fell to one knee, breathing harder than she expected.

She clutched at her chest and tried to will oxygen back into her lungs. "It's done. It's all done."

Cinderella used the sword to prop herself back to standing. With some difficulty, she walked straight ahead and through the puff of smoke that used to be her stepmother. It completely dissipated as she walked through it. She stepped past to what was now an empty throne and looked down at her fallen sister.

She shook her head. Kiyara was long gone, but there was a strange look upon the girl's face. She didn't look as though things had been cut short. She looked at peace. She looked as though, in the last moments of her life, she finally lived her truth.

"You were always my sister. That is how I'll remember you."

Gingerly at first, but then at an unwieldy gallop, Falstone emerged from behind the face of the sculpture he'd hidden behind. He placed his hand on the back of her neck. "I thought you were done for a second there. I think I owe you more than a few drinks, my lady."

Cinderella smirked. "I need a nap more than I need a drink." She looked back to the empty throne and around the expansive chamber. "Have you seen Braedon?"

Falstone's grief-stricken look spoke volumes. "I don't understand. I don't know what that witch did to him."

Cinderella rubbed the bridge of her nose. "The same thing she's done to so many others. But, at least she'll never do it again." She sighed. "Tell me where he is. I want to see him."

The hefty knight would make a terrible card player, as his eyes immediately betrayed the location of the prince. Cinderella kept the sword held high and walked quickly into the hallway. Her heart momentarily stopped when she saw him. The sword clattered loudly to the ground below.

Just outside the room, and in plain sight of the partygoers who had walked toward the ruckus of the throne room, were Malina and Braedon hand in hand. Her lips were pressed firmly against his.

CHAPTER 40

Cinderella rode home in a carriage across from Falstone. She was silent for most of it as she let the events of the last few hours sink in. Armenia had been defeated, but not without her stepmother giving Cinderella one last gift. Given how her father acted over the course of the past ten years, she wasn't sure if there was any chance of getting back the Braedon she knew.

The thief wasn't sure how she did it, but in that short time outside the throne room, Malina had secured a marriage proposal from the heartbroken soon-to-be king. The demon happily accepted. It was like her father's second marriage all over again.

From what she knew of the large knight across from her, he was quieter than normal as well. Much in the way she had been shunned, the bonds of friendship between him and the erstwhile prince had likewise been severed.

"He said he didn't know me. It was like the last few years never happened for him. I know they say that drinking causes memory loss, but this is something–"

"It's not your fault, Falstone. It's terrible and it's magical, but it's not your fault."

Falstone's eyes seemed to appreciate her compassion, but they betrayed his lack of belief. His guilt was deafening.

The carriage stopped when it reached Cinderella's home. With her dad barely able to speak a word, and her stepmother turned into smoke, she supposed she'd been upgraded from servant status.

She nodded toward Falstone. "Think of him more when you get some sleep. If you'd like to talk things over more, I'm happy to do so."

As she reached for the door, the sweaty knight stopped her. "Wait. Before... whatever it was... happened to him, Braedon gave me something for you."

Cinderella squinted, until she remembered that final dance with the prince. "The note."

He pulled the parchment from his jacket pocket. "I didn't read it. I wanted to, of course, but I actually never got the chance." He placed it in her palm. "Tell me what it says, after you've been able to... after you've gotten some rest."

She smiled. "You're a good friend. If he were in his right mind, he'd be very happy you did this for him."

Falstone jumped up from his seat and wrapped his arms around the thief. She squeezed him back.

"If you ever need someone to drown your sorrows with, you know exactly where I'll be."

Though she was in pain, the gesture of affection helped her feel warm. "I promise I'll take you up on it."

Cinderella stepped down from the carriage, her feet still bare from the battle. When she reached the ground, she turned to see Falstone blowing her a kiss. Then the carriage pulled off and left her there, alone. She looked down at the note and took a deep breath as she opened the parchment. She focused her eyes and squinted at the words that were highlighted by moonlight.

> *I'm sorry, Elle. The idea of magic had always been thwarted for me when there was nothing the entire kingdom could do to bring my father back. But I'm warming to the concept after seeing what the Godmother was able to coax out of me. Especially after seeing what happened with you and the sword in the blacksmith's house. But really, the greatest magic of all has been spending time with you. I hope you don't hate me, and I hope I have the opportunity to be in your company much more often. Besides, I have a feeling one of these days*

I'm going to beat you.
Love,
Braedon

Cinderella let herself read the words one more time before she allowed the parchment to slip from her fingers. A light midnight breeze carried the paper away from her, scuttling it across the cobblestone and out of her view. She walked inside the house and shut the door.

Cinderella lay there in her dress for an entire day. There were several moments when the pain, both mentally and physically, nearly abated enough to let her stand and change. That's when the thoughts of her sister or the engaged Braedon came to mind and forced her back down. According to her mother's former servants, news had spread quickly of the impending marriage. Not only that, but Braedon would be formally crowned king in his mother's absence. This would come shortly before Malina, the new love of his life, would become the Queen of Loren. It seemed as though Armenia's final wish would be fulfilled.

A part of the thief considered one last mission to rescue the prince from his fate. She knew that security around the castle would likely be tripled and that her efforts to get into the castle would be a suicide mission. But what exactly would she be rescuing him from? If her father was any indication, he'd be just as morose at the altar as he would on the run.

If he chose to leave the castle with her in the first place.

A full day after the battle with Armenia, Cinderella was still in her dress. She might have stayed in this condition for another few hours if she hadn't heard a noise from downstairs. They were footsteps. Someone was walking around the house, but who? At long last, the noises were enough to get Cinderella out of bed and into something more comfortable. She took one of her daggers with her, just in case.

As she stalked down the staircase, she realized there were two sets of voices downstairs.

One of them was her father's.

And he was laughing.

"By the gods."

As she turned at the corner, the sight before her was absolutely astounding. Her father stood in the middle of the kitchen with a look of pure joy upon his face. His hands were placed around the lower back of a woman who stood beside him. He was dancing. Cinderella didn't know whether to laugh or cry; then she saw her father twist, revealing his partner. Cinderella could nearly see through the ghostly version of the Godmother before her. She was laughing and smiling, too. But she was also beginning to fade away.

Cinderella felt frozen in place. Watching her father and mother share one last moment together was something she never believed possible.

"Magic really does exist."

The Godmother had almost faded out of existence when she placed her lips upon her husband's cheek. He closed his eyes, enraptured. With her final moment in hand, the Godmother looked toward Cinderella and smiled. The thief smiled back before the apparition of her mentor, her mother, and her friend disappeared from reality.

Cinderella's chest had never felt so open in her entire life. Revenge and pain that had bottled itself up for so long seemed to finally fade away. She was so lost in the moment that she almost didn't notice when her father sat down beside the kitchen table and gestured for his daughter to join.

"Come here, honey. We have to talk."

All her expectations had gone out the window. She didn't know what to expect anymore. She didn't know what to believe.

Cautiously, the thief stepped forward and took a seat next to her father. She nearly jumped out of her chair when he placed his hand on hers.

For the first time in a decade, the previously cold man looked at her with warmth. "I'm sorry."

"It wasn't your fault, Father."

He shook his head. "It doesn't matter. I'm not sure how your mother brought me back, but I'm not going to let it go to waste. I'm going to make up for it, and now we're going to be a father and a daughter. Is that okay? I would understand it if it was–"

Cinderella interrupted her father with a massive hug. She couldn't help but laugh and cry as she embraced him.

The next few days were a flurry of energy and activity in the village. Preparations for the prince's coronation and wedding were all that was on everybody's mind, including Cinderella's. At first, she tried to ignore it all. A deed had arrived two days after the ball that proved Cinderella's ownership of the Godmother's house. She hoped she would get one last glance at the woman who protected her for so long, but her mentor had vanished.

This was much to the chagrin of Falstone, who confessed his love for her mentor during Cinderella's one attempt to fulfill her promise that she'd get a drink with the old, crazy knight. Falstone had seemed over it by the time he had his sixth ale of the night, though. She conceded to having two drinks as she tried to put the prince and his fate out of her mind.

It was the day before the joint wedding and coronation, and Cinderella was listening to her father chattering away while he made dinner. Ever since he'd come back, the man was a nonstop source of stories about Cinderella as a little girl and her mother. For the most part, the joy of hearing his voice once again was almost enough to cover up the pain. As they were about to serve themselves, Cinderella heard a knock on the front door.

Her father raised an eyebrow. "Expecting company?"

She shook her head and pulled out her dagger. "No. I'm not."

Her father placed his hands on her hips. "Do you really have to take a dagger to the door with you every time you check to see who it is?"

She gave a little wink. "Yes. Yes, I do."

The thief walked softly toward the door and looked through the small hole to see who was there. Her pulse quickened when she spied a man she thought she'd never see again. Cinderella opened the door, and the prince brushed past her and into the house.

"Braedon?"

After he'd stepped into the house, the dead-eyed prince quickly turned on his heels and faced her. "Good evening." His voice remained an eerie monotone.

Cinderella's heart opened upon seeing him, but why on Earth would he be here?

"Don't you–don't you have something to be getting ready for?"

He cleared his throat. "I've been confused these last two days. My... heart is telling me something different from my head."

Cinderella noticed that Braedon had a small satchel thrown over one shoulder. He began to fish around inside it.

Until her father came back, Cinderella had never heard any of the men who'd been changed by Armenia say anything close to what Braedon had already spoken. The hope grew within her.

The prince pulled out something Cinderella recognized immediately. One of her shiny golden glass slippers from the ball.

She held her breath. "Why did you bring–"

"Can you try this on? I think it belongs to the woman I love."

Strange as it was to hear the word "love" without any feeling behind it, the thief stepped forward and took the shoe from Braedon's hand.

Everything seemed to slow down around her as she placed the slipper on the ground and let her foot slide into it. Just as it had been on the night of the ball, the glass slipper was a perfect fit.

When the prince looked down at Cinderella's foot, a red glow shined through his shirt. Cinderella looked at the light, and then up at Braedon's eyes. Within moments, the soulless stare that had accompanied his entire visit was gone. He blinked a few times, and like that, he was back. The prince gave his head a little shake and smiled.

Cinderella almost collapsed, barely keeping herself up by steadying her hand on the wall.

They both remained silent for a moment until Braedon lifted a necklace from under his shirt, a small piece of red jewel dangling at the end of it.

He took a step toward her. "Cinderella. I felt trapped in there, like I was trying to get out."

The thief let her hand run through her hair. "That's part of the Heartstone. How did you even get that? How did you know that it could protect you from her?"

Braedon took another step forward. "A little bird told me."

Cinderella's heart fluttered. "You think you're so funny."

His eyebrows danced. "I think my funniest act was ordering the guards in the castle to imprison my bride-to-be. Malina won't be a problem anymore."

Cinderella took a deep breath and stepped forward. They were now only inches apart.

She swallowed. "But there are already so many people in town waiting to celebrate. What are you going to tell them?"

Prince Braedon took Cinderella's hand and rubbed his fingers into her palm. The feeling was electric.

"I'll just have to say that we're celebrating something different."

The prince closed his eyes and leaned forward. Cinderella did the same and pressed her lips into his.

Every thought that she'd never be happy again retreated in an instant. The thief let herself lean into Braedon's body, as their mouths continued to show the way they felt.

It would be the first kiss of many.

About the Author

Casey Lane loves fairy tales, superheroes, and magic of all kinds. As the author of the Fairy Tales Forever series, Casey is grateful for the opportunity to spice up classic tales with some kickass heroines. Casey Lane is the pen name of a fiction and nonfiction author whose books have been downloaded nearly half a million times.

www.caseylanebooks.com

39514874R00103

Made in the USA
Middletown, DE
20 January 2017